Moon in Blue Eyes

Co-Editor - Neysa Kadam
Arvind Kadam

ISBN

Hardcase 979-8-89544-868-7
Paperback 979-8-89498-803-0

Table of Contents

Acknowledgements

I am not a writer. I believe it's not written by me, but by the blessings of Lord Shiva. I had not planned to write this book. The thoughts came to me, and the book was self-written.

I believe that a book is not written by a single person. It's true for me as well. There are many people who, consciously or unconsciously, supported me to write this book.

The first one are my parents, as nobody has loved me more, which is true for most of us. Their sacrifices have made me what I am today. This wouldn't have been possible without my parents' unconditional love and sacrifices for me.

My younger brother, Arun, and my younger sister, Aparna, are perhaps the greatest joys in my life. Their unconditional love and affection have always helped me to accept things as they are. They both are the most consistent source of support and joy in my life. I believe

I have done very good karma in my previous life to have them in this life.

My wife, Sandhya, who has brought great transformations in my life.

Children are the greatest joy for their parents, and I have been fortunate to have two of them. My son, Kshitij, is my life's first unconditional love, and I have been very fortunate to be his father. My younger daughter, Neysa, is my life's energy and joy. Every time I look at her, she gives me hope and strength to become a better person. I thank both of you for giving my life a beautiful purpose.

I can't go ahead without mentioning a few of my closest friends who have been my source of joy and happiness. The list is not exhaustive, but I want to personally thank Amit Gupta, Jayant Manhar, Vipin Kataria, Pawan Sawhney, Santosh Soni, Vibhor Mehra, Sanjay Sharma, Ashish Arora, Ankur Verma, Sudhir Kumar, Amit Tyagi, and Hitesh Negi. My life wouldn't be so joyful without your presence. Each one of you has immensely enriched my life.

Moon in Blue Eyes

The eyes are the gateway to the outer world, and to access the inner Universe, we must go inside… by closing our eyes. The eyes are the boundary that separates the visible outer world from the real inner Universe. A Universe that is loving, forgiving, accepting as we are, and giving abundant happiness and peace.

Beauty lies in the eye of the beholder, but what happens when the beholder is only looking with love and feeling only with his senses? Would it mean that the relevance of colour, creed, and sex matters when all that radiates is pure love, God?

You can have a beautiful life only when you have achieved a state of pure love, and caught a glimpse of God, radiating pure energy, Shiva, as we commonly call him with love.

Rishis/Munis have been informing us about Him and embracing Him with total acceptance, but we have eyes, and we know the value of everything.

Mahi

The evening sky was turning dark with ominous black clouds. It had never looked so dark before, as if light had abandoned planet Mahi.

There were loud thunderstorms, lighting up the whole dark forest. Incessant rain poured on Kumeru mountain as if to flood the entire mountain. All forest animals were running scared, seeking shelter from the incessant downpour from the sky. Everyone prayed for the rains to stop. The mountain rivers were flowing in full stream, violently carrying everything in their path. Water gushed from everywhere into the mountain rivers.

It looked as if the rain god, Indra, was angry and today would flood Mahi. Mahi cojoined brother of another planet, Prithvi. These two planets were together yet very far apart. They were born together but existed in different dimensions.

The large rock in the middle of the forest was special. It glowed faintly in darkness. It had a flat surface on its top and smooth edges running across its sides. It was part of a meteor which fell on Mahi millions of years ago. Some believed that it fell from heaven. Such a beautiful rock, which glows in darkness. No plant ever grew on that rock. From a distance, it looked out of place in the middle of all the greenery. It was revered by the forest inhabitants.

Suddenly, there was a burst of loud thunderstorms. The lightning struck that rock, and then dead silence fell. The rains and lightning stopped; only darkness enveloped Kumeru. A faint light glowed from the rock where a lean body of a young man was resting. The young man didn't look from this world. His face was glowing in darkness, emitting a kind of peace and happiness that this world desperately needed. The world, which was living in fear.

That young man's name was Abhay.

He was transported from another world to this isolated place in the middle of the forest. He looked human but didn't come from the human world. There was not a single human soul on Kumeru mountain. The mountain was inhabited by all kinds of animals, so-called wild by humans.

Vasu, the serpent king, was told about the arrival of the young man, Abhay. He only knew about the arrival but didn't know the day and time. Vasu was a very powerful serpent king. He lorded over the serpent city, Pataal

Lok. It was an underground serpent city. He himself took charge of watching the rock for the young man's arrival. Abhay was an important young man! When Abhay appeared on that rock, a few metres away, lying on the dark patch on a glowing grey rock, Vasu immediately slithered into the forest. Vasu had been on that rock's watch for a long time and knew whom to report. Time was not to be wasted.

A few minutes later, all kinds of forest animals were running towards that barren rock. All of them were looking at the young man, speechless to find him there. Their hope of a peaceful life was lying in front of them. His glowing face was radiating peace and hope. All their prayers were answered today. Some of them had moist eyes, looking up and thanking Lord Shiva.

All those eyes moved in the direction where a large ape family was walking towards the young man. They carried water in the makeshift leaf-pots in their large hands. Slowly, the ape leader, one named Virupaya, came and sat beside the young man. He slowly lifted the young man's head and kept it on his lap. It was like a mother gently taking care of her beloved child. He poured water on the young man's lips. Virupaya's large ape eyes showed a lot of devotion and respect. There was a small movement on the boy's face, showing signs of life.

After a while, the young man opened his eyes, sat, coughed loudly, and fell back on the lap. Virupaya lovingly held Abhay's head in his lap. After a few minutes, Abhay opened his eyes and sat up. He looked around. He wasn't sure where he was and why all those animals were looking at him with such love and devotion. Slowly, he looked at all those animals, and his eyes stopped at Virupaya who was sitting beside him on the rock. Virupaya, with happiness and devotion, had moist eyes and said,

"Dear, we have waited years for you to come to our abode. For years, we have kept a close watch on this rock for the moment of your arrival. There was a prophecy of a young man to come to our world, and his first appearance would be on this divine rock. You have arrived today to save us from the dark forces of Nansuki, who has been trying to annihilate our planet, Mahi. Last time, when we were on the verge of conquering those dark forces, it came with renewed force and destroyed our planet. We came to Kumeru mountain to save our lives and have been waiting here since that long."

Abhay didn't understand any of this and wondered why he didn't remember anything.

"Am I dreaming?"
"Am I hallucinating?"
"Who am I?"
"Where am I?"
"Why don't I remember anything?"
"Who are all these animals?"

All this thinking made his head throb hard, and he felt immense pressure on his chest, and he passed out again on that rock.

Abhay, a young boy in his early twenties, had a lean but muscular body. His face was shining and had the brilliance of a yogi. He had long flowing hair with sharp features. Wearing a white loincloth, his fit body looked as if from heaven. A look on his face, and you fall in love with the young man. Innocent, wise, and focused, that's how you would describe him.

A few hours later, when he opened his eyes, still trying to remember anything he heard or saw, he was lying on a cot made of soft grass. Looking around, he observed that he was in a small hut built on some large tree. He mustered all his strength, stood up, and walked to look out of the door. He saw that this hut was built on a very large tree. There were numerous similar huts in all directions on the branches everywhere.

He watched young ape children playing around the tree, and older ones were huddled all around the tree on different branches. All of them were looking at his hut with utmost devotion. They all believed in Abhay's divinity as a saviour.

From the distance, he saw that one large ape, the same one he saw on the forest rock, was coming towards his hut. He was jumping from one branch to another. A few other apes were following him with some baskets. Upon arriving near Abhay's hut, he entered with folded hands and said,

"Today is a very auspicious day that you have arrived in our village. It was prophesised a long time back that you would appear in our village. We have always kept a close watch on that rock for your arrival."

"Hmm," muttered Abhay.

"In the excitement, I forgot to tell you my name. I am your humble well-wisher, Virupaya. I am the ape king of this forest. This is our village on Kumeru mountain. This is our divine land where evil powers lose their magic. Mount Kumeru is surrounded by forests all around. You are on our planet, Mahi."

"Mahi? Kumeru?" Abhay puzzled.

"You will learn everything with time. I am very grateful to Lord Shiva for being your companion and teacher in your initial journey," Virupaya said while standing in front of Abhay.

His associates carried a variety of fruits in their wooden basket, and they kept the fruit baskets near the bed.

Virupaya continued, while standing tall, "Dear Abhay, please accept these fruits and take enough rest. Tomorrow morning, I will show you our forest, and we will explain everything to you."

Abhay nodded and picked some fruits from the nearby basket, starting to relish them as he felt deep hunger inside. After finishing them, Abhay said,

"Pardon me, dear, but maybe you have been misguided as I am no saviour, and I don't even remember anything about myself. You called me Abhay, but I don't know if I am Abhay."

Virupaya smiled calmly and replied,

"Last week, the three Great Rishis Anesh, Medha, and Shaurya visited us from Prithvi, and they told me that you would be arriving shortly here. Your arrival was prophesised years ago, and we have all been waiting for this day. You carry powers to save both planets, Prithvi and Mahi. You will remember everything with time, and we are all here to help you remember."

Confused Abhay sat on one of the small benches in the corner and tried hard to remember anything, but his mind was totally blank. He wondered how all those eyes looking at him with so much love, expectation, and devotion could be wrong. With so much blank thinking, he felt tired. Virupaya continued,

"We have kept some water and fruits for you. You can take rest now. I will come tomorrow early morning. I will show you around our forest and introduce you to our priest, Ramdas. We will also start your training, and slowly, with time, you will remember everything."

Abhay nodded in agreement and decided to rest his throbbing head. Maybe sleep will clear his mind, and he will remember something about himself.

Virupaya left the hut with his associates, leaving Abhay alone in his hut with his thoughts.

Lying on the soft grass bed, he kept thinking about himself, got tired, and dozed off.

Abhay found himself in the middle of a dark, ominous forest which was being engulfed by fire. There was no life in that forest, no birds, no animals, no insects, just darkness everywhere. He saw the fire moving towards him, eating up every tree in its path. There was nothing he could do to stop it. The searing heat began to engulf him, burning his body from the inside out. Desperate, he started to run, trying to escape the flames and save himself. In the distance, he saw a lush, green mountain with tall trees, shrouded in dark clouds. He sprinted towards it, running faster and faster, driven by fear. Looking behind, the fire was running towards him, and suddenly he saw an ominous face coming out of the fire, shouting in a loud, thunderous voice,

"You can't run away from me. I am your end," he said, laughing loudly.

He reached the top of the mountain. The fire was engulfing the mountain from all sides. He had nowhere else to go. He felt being burned alive. He screamed louder and louder.

He woke from his sleep, perspiring and bewildered about his dream. He watched Virupaya hurriedly coming inside his hut, and he put his palm on Abhay's head and said,

"I heard your screams and ran here. You are very warm. What happened? What did you see in your dream?"

Abhay told him about the dream and asked Virupaya if there was any meaning to his dream. Virupaya had a long, pensive look at Abhay and said,

"Nothing happens without reason. Nothing will ever happen to you without any reason. The dream was a reminder of your karma, a reminder to tell you about the powers inside you. Power, which can move mountains, destroys mountains, and even planets."

"I don't remember any powers inside me,"

"You will."

"What if you are wrong about me? What if I am an ordinary person who has lost his memory?"

Virupaya said gravely, "Nansuki has already sensed your presence. Your dream is a reminder of that. An ordinary person will have ordinary dreams. We need to be careful. We don't have much time to train you. Your body needs rest. I am outside if you need anything."

Before leaving, he said,

"Get ready early in the morning and meet me downstairs on the ground. We will go to the Lord Shiva temple in the forest and start your training."

Lying down on his bed, Abhay tried to sleep, but questions kept on cropping up in his mind.

"Who am I?"
"My name is Abhay?"
"From where have I come?"
"Who is Nansuki?"
"Why is everyone thinking that I am their saviour?"
"Do I have any powers?"
"Why don't I remember anything?"

Pondering over all these questions, he slept after some time.

Soon, the whole ape village on that tree was fast asleep. Some were happy and satisfied that their Lord Shiva had heard their prayers. Pleased with their prayers, Lord Shiva had finally sent their saviour. With happy looks on their faces, the ape village slept peacefully that night.

The news of Abhay's arrival spread like wildfire on Mount Kumeru and the surrounding forests. There was a sense of relief among all animals. Finally, their saviour, had arrived on Mount Kumeru.

– 2 –

Temple

The Lord Shiva temple in the middle of a dense forest was a stone structure. It was believed that the ancient rishis did great tapasya[1] in this temple millennia ago. During their tapasya, their pious aura cleansed the whole forest of negative energies. The pious energy from their tapasya trickled from this temple and surrounded the whole mountain. To this day, black magic loses all its powers; the moment they step on this mountain.

Outside the temple, Nandi bull's stone statue facing the Shiva Linga was located. Nandi is always in an attention position, ready to be called by Lord Shiva. It is believed that no ceremony of Lord Shiva is complete without first being prayed to Nandi. Inside the temple, there was a Shiva Linga of black stone in a small chamber. It was decorated with wildflowers, and a small lamp was burning. A brass utensil was hanging on the top of the Shiva Linga, dripping water slowly. It smelled serene, ancient, and peaceful. The inside walls of the

---

1   Tapasya – great penance by rishis

chamber were made of large black stones. The stones were engraved with various forms of Lord Shiva and Goddess Parvati. Some of the engravings showed Lord Shiva's children, Lord Ganesh, and Lord Kartikeya.

The temple was surrounded by a serene atmosphere. The cacophony of birds was all around the temple, which lived on the surrounding fruit-bearing trees. When Abhay and Virupaya reached the temple, they saw an old man standing at the entrance steps wearing a two-piece priest's clothing. The priest was of short height, wore traditional saffron cloth dress, and had a radiant face full of wisdom. Smiling with folded hands, the priest welcomed Abhay and said,

"I feel very fortunate to meet you, and I have waited for this day for a long time. With Lord Shiva's blessings, my life's wish is fulfilled."

By this time, Abhay was getting used to being welcomed by strangers with love and devotion. But why they did so was something he hadn't figured out yet.

"Respected Ramdas, I am also very fortunate to meet you. Virupaya told me about you while coming here. I believe that the village is fortunate to have such a learned priest working for their betterment. I would be glad to learn from you," Abhay replied with folded hands.

"Virupaya and the forest inhabitants are very kind. They shower so much love and affection on me, which I don't truly deserve."

Both smiled with affection, appreciating each other's humble nature.

Ramdas continued, "I have arranged a small ceremony to welcome you. Please join me inside the temple and take Lord Shiva's blessings."

All entered the temple and sat around the Shiva Linga.

Ramdas performed a short prayer praising Lord Shiva for his blessings on both worlds, Kumeru and Abhay. After the prayers, they offered milk, water, honey, and ghee[2], on the Shiva Linga.

After completing the prayer in the temple, they came out of the temple. Ramdas invited Abhay to sit on the stone steps at the temple entrance. Virupaya, joyfully looking at Abhay, said,

"Dear Abhay, let me introduce our priest, Ramdas. He is our spiritual guide and an ocean of wisdom. He had told us a long time back that your arrival was imminent. Vasu, the serpent king, was requested to keep an eye on the rock so that he could bring you safely to our village."

Abhay, still confused, didn't understand any of this and was looking forward to making sense of what was happening around him.

---

2   Ghee – clarified butter

Ramdas looked at Abhay thoughtfully and said, "Last month, the three Great Rishis visited me. They told me that their yagna was bearing fruit and was about to finish shortly. They told me that the cosmic rock in the forest was the only place on this mountain which would be able to absorb the energy of your arrival. From that day, Vasu was guarding the rock. Yesterday's great deluge and abnormal lightning was an indication that there is some imbalance of energy on Mahi. They were correct that at the right time you would appear on that rock."

Abhay, trying to make any sense of this, asked, "Dear Ramdas, I am extremely sorry, but I am unable to understand anything you just said. In fact, I don't remember anything about myself. Is it possible that you might be wrong about me?"

Ramdas smiled and said, "Dear Abhay, the whole Universe is dynamic in nature, and the energy is continuously flowing through the Universe. We try to make sense of it using the movement of stars and constellations. The three Great Rishis are experts in decoding the Universe's language. They are the keepers of balance in both worlds. Please have patience, and with time, you will remember your true self."

Abhay looked at Virupaya and Ramdas' faces. They were innocent, wise, and devoted towards Abhay.

Sometimes, when we don't have answers, we need to trust and believe in something bigger than us. When we start our journey, maybe the path is invisible, but belief in oneself can lift us to achieve greater heights. During the dark times, we remember our true hidden self.

Abhay had to keep the trust. It will show him the path when the time comes.

Abhay asked them, "Please forgive my impatience. I am very grateful to you both. Can you please tell me when my teachings and training will start? I want to know everything."

Ramdas calmly replied, "We have just finished a small ceremony to start your teachings, with God's blessings. I will help you learn the scriptures. Virupaya will introduce you to village people and others in this forest. He will also train you in various fighting techniques and handling weapons. I will start the yagna for your victory. It would also give us celestial weapons which you would use during the war."

"That would be a good start for me," Abhay hurriedly replied.

"We will take our leave now. Before showing him our village and introducing him to other people in the forest, I will take Abhay to see our divine tree, *Mangal*," Virupaya said, standing up eagerly.

"That's a very good idea. I was about to tell you to visit the *Mangal* tree with Abhay. That would be a very auspicious way to start his training," Ramdas calmly replied.

Virupaya nodded and asked Abhay to follow him.

Virupaya took Abhay into the dense area of the mountain. After walking for half an hour, they reached a water stream which was flowing from the top of the mountain. The water was ice-cold, and they didn't want to touch it. They crossed it by jumping on large stones in the middle of the stream. After crossing the water stream, Virupaya said,

"Can you see that rock behind that tall jamun tree?"

"Yes, slightly. I can hardly see it clearly. It's covered behind a lot of bush," Abhay, trying to focus on it, replied.

While briskly climbing towards that rock, Virupaya said, "Correct. We just have to climb and go across the jamun tree. There is a small cave opening behind it. Inside the cave, there is our auspicious Mangal tree."

Abhay, walking behind Virupaya, replied, "Oh, looks like not many people come to this side of the forest."

Looking back at Abhay, Virupaya said, "That's true. It's in an isolated area of the forest. Only people with a spiritual bend of mind prefer to come here."

"Why?" asked Abhay with a surprised look.

"Evolution happens at three levels: physical, intellectual, and spiritual. Physical and intellectual evolutions happen due to external events, but spiritual evolution happens from inside, a desire to merge with the One. You can show the direction, but you can never force someone to light the fire of spiritual evolution."

Abhay heard and understood the meaning of Virupaya's statement. Virupaya was an able soldier, captain, leader, and highly evolved spiritual person. He was relieved to think that he would enjoy his training under such an able leader.

They climbed a few metres up and crossed the large jamun tree. There were a few rocks scattered around the area. Virupaya looked for the medium-sized rock and called Abhay,

"The entrance of this cave is very narrow. There is no place to walk. We need to crawl inside. Be careful of the loose stones in the cave," explained Virupaya, while motioning Abhay to follow him inside the cave.

Carefully, they crawled for a few metres inside and crossed the narrow pathway. It was not an easy crawl as it was filled with sand and small rocks. Inside the cave, they found themselves in a very large hall.

It was a mesmerising view, out of this world. It looked like a beautiful painting in an alien world. In the middle of the cave, there was a huge banyan tree. The cave ceiling above the tree had a large hole, and the tree had grown beyond the cave opening. The sun rays came through the leaves and scattered around the cave. One could see floating dust particles in the sun rays. The tree was glowing in the cave, absorbing the sunlight and sending it in all directions of the cave. There was no other plantation in the entire cave, except the banyan tree in the middle.

The atmosphere in the cave was calm and serene. It also smelled ancient. There was a faint sound coming from the tree. Abhay tried to listen and faintly heard,

"Om Namay Shivay."

Someone was meditating in the cave. Tree?

Virupaya came near the tree and, with folded hands, whispered a silent prayer. Abhay also followed him, and both sat cross-legged in a meditative pose under the tree. They sat silently for more than an hour in a meditative pose.

After an hour, Virupaya opened his eyes and saw Abhay in deep meditation. His face was glowing like a tree's glow. He called his name slowly, and Abhay opened his eyes after some time.

Virupaya, thoughtfully looking at the tree, told Abhay, "Thousands of years ago, there was a rishi who was a great devotee of Lord Shiva. He had travelled from

Prithvi. He was looking for a quiet place to meditate, wanting to meditate for years without any disturbance. After travelling all over Mahi, he stumbled upon this cave by mistake. Passing over this cave, he accidentally fell inside from the top hole. He loved the silence in this cave so much that he decided to meditate here. Over the years, a banyan tree grew underneath the rishi. It is believed that the rishi is still meditating inside the tree's trunk. He is still unaware that he is inside the tree. His wish of undisturbed peace was fulfilled by Lord Shiva by placing him inside the tree trunk. Anyone who meditates under this tree gets the rishi's blessings, and all his wishes are fulfilled."

Abhay heard Virupaya with his eyes closed and replied,

"Thank you for bringing me here. It is indeed a pious place and takes away all worries. I feel blessed and energised after meditating here."

After looking silently at the tree for a few minutes, they stood up calmly. Both walked towards the tree and placed their hands on it. The tree trunk was cold. They felt that the tree was slightly pulsating, and gradually the vibrations started increasing. With surprised looks, both stepped back, looking at the tree. Something extraordinary was happening in the tree. The ground also started vibrating, and they didn't understand what was happening. Whatever was happening at that moment, it didn't scare them. There was still a sense of security and warmth in the cave.

The tree trunk started to glow brightly. Virupaya and Abhay covered their eyes with their hands as they were unable to see anything in such bright light. It was as if the sun had risen from the tree. Slowly, a rishi appeared from that bright light.

He wore a saffron loincloth draped over his lean body, with rudraksha beads adorning his neck and wrist. Though he had no physical form, his presence was projected from the tree.

He looked at both Abhay and Virupaya and, in a booming voice, he said,

"I meditated in this cave for hundreds of years. For years, I have felt people coming into this cave meditating with me. I have always blessed those who meditated with me here. For the first time, I felt that I was in the presence of Lord Shiva. Abhay, I am glad that you came here and meditated with me. Over the years, I have been blessed to transcend my physical self. With the grace of Lord Shiva, I bless your physical body to become so strong that no weapon or animal can hurt it. You will be immune to enemies' weapons."

Saying this, rays of energy poured from the rishi's eyes and entered Abhay's body. Abhay's body brightened up. He felt power surge throughout his body, rejuvenating every cell in his body.

The rishi, with a calm smile, looked at Abhay and continued,

"I bless you both, and may Lord Shiva bless you with victory in the coming war, and all your enemies are defeated."

Abhay folded his hands in front of the rishi and said,

"I am very grateful for your blessing. I feel very fortunate to have seen you. May Lord Shiva fulfil all your wishes."

The rishi looked at Virupaya and smiled. He knew that he was in front of divinity. Slowly, the rishi's image merged again in the tree.

Virupaya looked at Abhay and happily said,

"That's the most beautiful thing that happened to me in this life. All because of you."

Abhay smiled, and they both started to walk towards their village.

Memories

Ramdas then began to talk about Nansuki, a powerful demon who threatened both planets. "The three Great Rishis Anesh, Medha, and Shaurya had performed yagna (worship) to Lord Shiva and Goddess Parvati for more than a decade. Nansuki was a powerful evil, and the three Great Rishis' powers to subdue him were ineffective. Nansuki's terror on both worlds was so great that it threatened both planets' survival. The three Great Rishis performed a great yagna to please Lord Shiva and Goddess Parvati to seek a path to defeat Nansuki. He was so powerful that even we have been forced to stay on this mountain, away from his black magic power. Nansuki was cursed by an ancient Great Rishi to lose all his powers the moment he steps on this mountain. He keeps on sending his disciples to attack us, but we have always conquered his disciples. On Mahi, this mountain is the only place that is safe from his attacks."

Ramdas continued with a calm posture,

"Lord Shiva and Goddess Parvati blessed our three Great Rishis. After getting pleased by their devotion and yagna, they granted a boon, and both of you were born. You are a part of their energy to rescue Prithvi and Mahi from the evil Nansuki, who is hell-bent on destroying both worlds."

After pondering over what was told, Abhay stood up and asked if they both believed that he could fight an evil force like Nansuki, who is so powerful that even gods tremble before him. Ramdas removed the rudraksha mala [3]from his left wrist and, while placing it in his right hand, said,

"You are a part of both Lord Shiva and Goddess Parvati, and there is no power bigger in the Universe than them. You are born to rescue us, but you need to remember your true power. I am initiating powerful yagnas from tonight, and Virupaya will start your training in celestial weapons from today. We hope that you will be ready before Nansuki escapes from his prison."

Abhay calmly asked,

"If you believe that I am born to defeat Nansuki and free both worlds from his terror, then I am willing to go through the training and remember my true self. I am thankful to both of you for believing in me and showing me the path."

---

3   Mala - rosary

Looking at Virupaya, Abhay continued,

"I believe priest Ramdas doesn't need us for his yagna. We need to go and start fight training. There is no need to waste more time,"

Virupaya, with folded hands, thanked Ramdas and took Abhay to the training ground, which was a few minutes away. The training ground was built in the middle of the forest on the sloping side of the mountain. Wind blew from the nearby valley at high speed towards the training ground. It was not an easy area for archery as the direction and speed of the wind were unpredictable. On the distant tree in the corner, there was a small round-shaped wooded board with concentric circles. The wooded board was hanging by a rope and was constantly moving with the breeze. Virupaya folded his hands and muttered a small silent prayer on his lips. After a few minutes, he opened both his arms forward, and a bow appeared in his hands. Abhay also saw a quiver appear on Virupaya's shoulders with only one arrow. Drawing the arrow towards the mark, Virupaya shot the arrow, and it hit the centre of the wooden target. Abhay was very impressed as the mark was approximately five hundred metres away and remarked,

"It looks difficult to hit a moving target from such a distance,"

Smiling, Virupaya offered his bow and quiver to Abhay and asked him to try. Abhay took it from Virupaya and pulled the string, concentrating on the target, and shot. Hearing some leaves rustle, he saw that the arrow hardly crossed half the distance and fell on the ground. Virupaya smiled and said,

"When I tried for the first time, I couldn't even load the arrow on the bowstring. You have done well for the first try," Abhay tried to hide his embarrassment and said.

"You effortlessly hit the target, and I couldn't even reach the target. Can you teach me so that I can hit like you?"

Virupaya nodded and said,

"Any skill can be learned when you have patience and practice well. A teacher can only guide his student, but perseverance, dedication, and devotion to your teacher can help you learn any skills."

Virupaya took Abhay closer to the target and said,

"Practice from a close distance and hit the target, and slowly increase the distance. Once you get trained hitting from a distance, then we will start practising on riding a horse. With your dedication and perseverance, you should be a skilled archer in no time. But remember, you don't have the luxury of time. Nansuki has already sensed your presence."

Virupaya corrected Abhay's posture and asked him to practice. He stood behind Abhay and watched him hitting the target board. Abhay started practising, and after a few hours, he came to Virupaya and said,

"I have been practising for hours, but still I couldn't hit the target even once. Looks like I need a lot of training," Virupaya nodded and said,

"First, perfect the posture. Once your posture is correct, then concentrate on the centre of the target board. While concentrating on the board, observe only the red mark. Your concentration should be only in the centre of the board. When you practice well hitting the centre board, slightly keep on increasing the distance. Soon, you would be able to hit the centre from the distance."

"It's all about the practice and practice," Abhay repeated, charged up.

"Correct."

"Thanks."

"Abhay, the sun is about to set. Let's go back and have dinner. A lot of people want to see and meet you."

Virupaya took back his bow and quiver, and with closed eyes, said a silent prayer. His bow and quiver disappeared from his hands.

While walking back, Abhay, with a little surprised look, asked,

"Can I ask you about the bow and arrow?" How does it come to you and disappear? I observed that the quiver had only one arrow, which comes back to the quiver as soon as it hits the target."

Virupaya smiled. "We have celestial weapons," he said, "granted to us by the rishis. Some are very powerful, and some are used for simple tasks like training new archers. When you are ready, you will also get them based on your training."

The weather was getting a little chilly, with a little fog engulfing them. Looking at the ground near the mountain foot, Abhay asked,

"You mentioned the magical powers of Kumeru. Even Nansuki can't come here. Is it true?"

Virupaya replied,

"That's true. Some ancient rishis had performed a lot of tapasya on this mountain. For a few centuries, they even made Kumeru their ashram to train their disciples. Over time, their tapasya percolated down into the mountain. It became impervious to any kind of black magic. This mountain is so pure that anyone with malafide intentions or black magic loses all their power as they step on this mountain. This is the safest place for us on Mahi."

"Really?"

"We have never been attacked by Nansuki or his disciples on this mountain. Although the forests around the mountain are filled with Nansuki's disciples. As soon as they step on the mountain, they lose all their black magic powers."

Abhay was thinking that he had learned so much in a single day and was wondering how many secrets still needed to be unfolded. His head started throbbing again with the thoughts.

"Who is Nansuki, and why is everyone so scared of him?"

Maybe his answers will be revealed soon.

The ape village was built on interconnected large trees. The strong branches, intervening with one another, created a safe place above the ground. There were a few huts built on branches, but mainly for specific purposes. Most of the apes stayed and slept on open branches. It was a very secure surrounding for apes.

After reaching his hut, Abhay started ravishing the fruits laid out for him. After eating to full stomach, he dropped onto his grass bed, wondering what else is in store for him tomorrow.

There was a giant fire-breathing snake attacking their village. He saw it burning trees, apes, priests, and children. Everyone was screaming his name and asking him to rescue them. It was a chilling atmosphere, and suddenly everyone fell silent. Abhay saw the fiery, fearsome eyes looking at him. He couldn't move his body; he tried to scream but couldn't utter a word. The snake flew towards him, and he woke up, perspiring profusely.

Abhay sat up, perspiring in the chilly weather.

Virupaya had just come near his hut and was sitting near the entrance. Abhay, worriedly, asked,

"What is happening? Whenever I try to sleep, I get the same dream of fire burning me."

Virupaya, while picking up a small branch, calmly looked at Abhay and said,

"He has sensed you. You need to learn to control those dreams. It will take some time, but you will. Ramdas has come to meet you. He is waiting for you downstairs. I believe he carries a message for you. Take your time to relax your mind and meet us down."

Abhay took some time to relax his heartbeat, which was beating at an unbelievably high rate. He washed his face with water and climbed down.

As soon as Ramdas saw Abhay, he excitedly said,

"I had a vision of our great three rishis, and they will arrive and meet you soon. They have asked me to start yagnas to get celestial weapons for you. I believe your archery training under Virupaya is going well. My disciples have collected all material for yagna. You can take a bath and come to the temple after an hour. We plan to start the yagna tonight as today is a very auspicious day," saying this Ramdas hurriedly left and vanished into the forest. Virupaya smiled and looked at Abhay and said,

"Training going well!" and grinned.

Abhay smiled and said, "Training has just started today. You said that I was doing well. At least, I can fire the arrows towards the target, unlike you who couldn't even fire the arrows."

Both laughed heartily.

After an hour, Abhay and Virupaya joined the initiating ceremonies in the temple. The yagna fire was lit outside the temple. Ramdas's assistants had prepared everything beforehand. Ramdas initiated the yagna in the name of Lord Shiva and Goddess Parvati. It was supposed to last a few days continuously. After the yagna initiation, Virupaya signalled Abhay to silently leave the yagna. Abhay, without making any noise, slowly stood up and left for the training ground.

After the gruelling day-long training, Abhay came back late in the evening. As soon as he rested on his grass bed and closed his eyes.

"Abhay, wake up and come to me. Find me. I am waiting for you."

Abhay heard a female voice calling his name. He immediately opened his eyes and saw that nobody was around. He stood up and peeked outside his door, and he didn't see anyone. Everyone was asleep in the middle of the night. Maybe he dreamt in his sleep. His body was tired, and he decided to take rest before another gruelling day ahead.

His eyes opened to the cacophony of morning birds. He woke up and met Virupaya under the tree playing with children. He observed that Virupaya was highly revered by other apes, and children loved to play with him. Apes from all around the nearby forests were visiting him continuously. They were coming to give him either some information or ask for some favours. Most of the internal colony issues were resolved by Virupaya without any violence.

Virupaya was in the middle of a meeting involving two warring ape colonies. Those colonies shared a boundary, and they often fought over common territories for food. Both colony leaders, with their close colony ministers, were sitting in front of Virupaya. Looking at Abhay, he asked him to sit beside him.

The warring colony leaders were called Pankaj and Alok. They were fighting over the mango trees between their colonies.

Pankaj said to Virupaya,

"Dear Virupaya, Alok's colony is overusing the mango trees. We have been peacefully eating mangoes without any problem for decades. Now we don't find any mangoes on trees as Alok's colony picks all ripe mangoes before our colony gets a chance to eat. It has never happened before, and this year, we have got very fewer mangoes for our colony."

Virupaya asked Alok, "

"Alok, is Pankaj telling the truth?"

"No, we don't trouble them. They are lazy, and by the time they come to pick up ripe mangoes, all are taken by our colony because they arrive early in the morning."

Pankaj said, "It has never happened before, but this year the mango growth was good. Still, we are not getting any for ourselves."

Abhay observed that this blame game would go on and walked towards the ape babies to play with them.

After some time, Virupaya also joined him, and they both started playing with children. The ape children were very fond of Abhay as he regularly brought fruits for them. He also loved telling them funny stories from the forest. After a few minutes, they both nodded to each other and left the village for the training ground.

With practice, Abhay was getting better at holding the bow and was able to hit the target a few times. Virupaya stood behind Abhay and watched him practice. He told him to work on his posture again and observe the wind flow direction. The wind flow direction needed to be considered for successfully hitting the target. Virupaya left after watching Abhay and told him that he would come in the late afternoon. Upon his return in the late afternoon, he watched Abhay practising and said,

"Today, you have improved your posture, and it is helping you to pull the string better. With time, you will be able to hit the target consistently."

"I know, it's not easy to practice. The posture, moving target, and wind flow. I need to observe everything," Abhay said while pulling the bowstring and concentrating on the target. This time, the arrow hit the wooden board on the outermost circle.

Gesturing to Abhay with his hand, Virupaya said, "Let's call it a day and go home. On the way, we must meet priest Ramdas."

They saw Ramdas busy in the yagna and didn't see them coming. Without disturbing Ramdas, they decided to walk back home.

Kumeru was a middle-sized mountain in the middle of a dense forest. There were multiple varieties of fruit trees which fed a large variety of animals and birds. Ample rainwater streams ran throughout Kumeru. It was a very serene and peaceful life.

The ape colony was located around the mountain top as it had the tallest trees in the forest. The height gave the apes an added advantage to keep a vigil around the mountain. For hundreds of miles, it was all dense forest, and rivers flowed out in the forest.

Who could have thought that such a calm forest was full of dangerous animals who could slice a man in one strike? It was rumoured that a few evil disciples of Nansuki were patiently waiting for his return in the forests down below.

While walking back, they heard feeble shouts from a distance and tried to locate the source of that noise. It was getting a little dark, but apes have a far better sense of smell and hearing. Trying to hear the sound's location, Virupaya said,

"I think there is some trouble in the forest below. This time of the season, there are melons in the forest, and some ape families go there for those melons. I hope it's only a wild beast and nothing dangerous. You go ahead and stay in the village, and I will go and check in the forest."

Angrily, Abhay said, "I can't go back to the village and leave you alone in danger. I will go with you, and if you all believe in what I am capable of, then probably you need me more than you realise."

Virupaya firmly said, "You are not ready. I need to take care of you until you are ready."

Abhay looked straight into Virupaya's eyes and said adamantly, "I will not leave you alone."

Looking into Abhay's eyes without any fear and with absolute confidence, Virupaya thought to himself, *Abhay wouldn't leave me alone in any danger.*

Virupaya said, "Follow me and don't get lost in the forest. The forest outside Mount Kumeru is full of dangerous animals. It might not be safe for you if you lose your way."

They both started running towards the feeble screams, which were getting louder. They ran fast and passed Kumeru in a few minutes. They were running towards the melon plantation and saw a few apes running towards them. They found one of the apes running towards them with deadly fear in its eyes and said,

"We have never seen such a large and powerful bull in our life. They came out of nowhere and started attacking us. I saw only one with my own eyes and ran away from there. Please go and save the others."

Saying this, he ran towards the mountain with terror in his eyes. Hearing this, Virupaya stood still, with anger in his eyes, and said a silent prayer. He then got a large bow and quiver on his shoulder. Taking out the arrow from the quiver, he started running towards the attack, followed by Abhay.

From a distance, they watched an ape being mauled by a fearsome large bull with its large horns. Immediately drawing his arrow, Virupaya shot. The arrow flew swiftly and hit the bull's right shoulder, but to their surprise, it fell with just a little scratch on the bull's shoulder. Virupaya was surprised to see the little scratch by its arrow, said, "It's not possible that a normal wilder beast is unscathed by my celestial arrow. This bull is no ordinary bull. You run towards the mountain. He will not be able to attack you on Kumeru as he would lose his magical powers."

Saying this, Virupaya started running towards the beast and shooting it with his arrows. The arrows were all falling on the ground without hurting the bull in any meaningful way.

When they came closer, the bull pulled Virupaya on his horns and threw him away. The bull looked at Abhay with menacing eyes and started running towards him. It all happened so fast that Abhay couldn't see where Virupaya fell. In a dilemma to save Virupaya first, Abhay charged towards the wilder beast, and both jumped towards each other.

Virupaya, from the distance, watched in horror with an open mouth. He stood up and started running towards the fighting. As he came closer, he was surprised to see the wilder beast lying dead on the ground with its neck broken. On top of the beast was Abhay standing with fire in his eyes and a fiery glow around his body. Coming closer to Abhay, Virupaya fell on his knees and with folded hands said,

"Oh my Lord, thanks a lot for being our saviour. I always knew that I was in the presence of some extraordinary power. Please accept me as your disciple and give your disciple a place at your feet. Please accept my apologies for not realising your true self." He started crying softly, with eyes full of love and devotion. Walking down from the beast, Abhay looked lovingly at Virupaya and comfortingly said, "You are my friend and my first teacher. Your place is not at my feet but in my heart." Abhay pulled Virupaya close and hugged him lovingly, looking at his face.

At a distance, another bull appeared, larger and more menacing. Virupaya and Abhay also looked at the bull. The bull looked at the dead bull, surprised and a little scared. Abhay and the bull locked their eyes, and suddenly the bull moved back and started running back into the jungle, scared for his life as if it had seen death itself.

Virupaya worriedly remarked, "Nansuki knows you are here."

Slowly, other apes started gathering around them with joy and came near Abhay. All of them surrounded Abhay and kissed his hand, saying a little prayer on their lips.

After reaching their village, the word spread that Abhay killed a monster bull with just one hand strike. Sitting on a large stone, he was surrounded by the whole village. All eyes were looking at him with love and devotion as if they were sitting in front of some God. Virupaya spoke about the battle in the forest and Abhay's courage and supernatural powers, how the other bulls ran away. Abhay closed his eyes; he heard his name being called by the same female voice. He opened his eyes, looked around but didn't find anyone around.

- 4 -

Giant Fish

Abhay's training started with new vigour. His archery practice improved every day. He was able to hit targets from far away. Spending a lot of time practising, he was getting better daily. He started riding Virupaya's horse for target practice. In any battle, warriors move fast on their horses and need to be trained to hit moving targets. He had placed a wooden board with red concentric circles hanging on a tree branch.

He stood far away to hit in the centre of the wooden board. He pulled the string and, with full force, he let go of the arrow. The arrow hit the centre mark. He pulled another arrow. As soon as he let the arrow fly towards the target, he saw someone from behind had hit the rope of the wooden board. The wooden board fell, and his arrow missed the target board. Surprised, he looked behind and saw Virupaya grinning.

Coming towards Abhay, he said,

"You still have to get better than your teacher. You still have a lot to learn."

Saying this, Virupaya laughed heartily. Abhay frowned at him and said, "I have practised for only a few weeks, and your practice is a few decades old. It's a matter of time. Soon, I will leave you behind."

Abhay started walking towards the wooden board to hang it again. He wanted to practice more and get better than Virupaya. His fight with the monster bull in the forest had renewed his commitment. He knew that he was born for a special purpose and he should never fail himself or the people around him. He always felt good after long, tiring practice.

When he came back after hanging the wooden board, Abhay saw Virupaya happily grinning. Surprised by Virupaya's grin, he asked,

"What on Mahi have you got to grin so broadly?"

With secret looks, Virupaya replied, "I've got a surprise for you."

Abhay frowned and looked at Virupaya and said, "What kind of surprise?"

Virupaya took out a small cloth from his pocket and said, "First, I need to blindfold you, and then you have to guess."

Abhay, with a surprised smile, agreed to blindfold him. After Virupaya blindfolded him, he held his arm and led him outside the training ground. Outside the training ground, he took him behind the tall trees.

Virupaya pulled Abhay's hand and put it on the side of an animal.

"Can you guess what this is?" asked Virupaya.

Abhay put his hand on the animal and patted it. The horse neighed softly. With excitement, Abhay removed his blindfold and jumped happily, with joy, and said,

"Wow, this is such a lovely horse. Where did you get it from?

Virupaya smiled and said,

"Ramdas was performing a wish-granting yagna. Yesterday, he was granted a horse. It is called Vayu, and it can run faster than any other animal. He wanted to come himself to deliver, but he can't leave the yagna unattended. He has sent Vayu with me for you. He has requested to come in the evening. He is expecting some powerful celestial weapon for you before he finishes the yagna. After finishing today's practice, come to my camp, and we will go together."

"Sure."

Vayu was unlike any other horse he had seen recently. It was pure white, much larger in size than the normal horses, confident, and muscular. Abhay lovingly patted Vayu on the head. Vayu took his touch lovingly and stepped back a little, levade, and started galloping around the ground at high speed. Abhay chuckled and started running towards the centre and watched Vayu running around at great speed. After a few rounds of galloping around, Vayu trotted towards Abhay, hugging lovingly. Abhay patted him and mounted on its back. Neighing and galloping, Vayu moved around the forest at great speed. Abhay was feeling as if he was flying in the air. The cold air was flowing through his flowing hair and face. With closed eyes, he was enjoying every moment. After some time, they came near a clean water lake. The water was so crystal clear that he could see the bottom of the lake. Different colours of stones were lying at its bottom, and various species of multiple colours of fish could be seen swimming. Abhay sat on the stone near the stream, and Vayu drank from the stream. After his stomach was full, Vayu started grazing grass around the stream.

Abhay could see Kumeru from a distance, covered in clouds. They had travelled far away in a short time. He remembered everyone in the colony and thought, why do such nice people fear Nansuki? Who in their right mind would want to threaten people like Ramdas and Virupaya? He shrugged and thought, maybe it's a problem for another day. Today, he wants to swim in this crystal clear water and have a nice bath. The lake was calling him to take a swim.

He walked towards the lake and jumped. The cold water struck his body sharply, causing him to shiver slightly as he swam with powerful butterfly strokes. His long hair clung to his neck and shoulders as he made his way to the middle of the lake, which was a few metres deep. He enjoyed the cold water against his skin, feeling it wash away the aches from his long days of practice. He started feeling refreshed after half an hour of swimming. The top of the mountain was covered with snow all year round. He felt the melting snow was filling this stream with such cold water. Vayu on his side, he made a mental note to come here regularly to refresh after practice hours.

A large dark shadow underwater was lurking away in the distance. The shadow was closely watching Abhay. After a while, the shadow started swimming very fast towards him. While swimming, Abhay noticed some dark shadow movement, and before he could change his direction, he saw a giant black fish attack him from below, jumping in the air to swallow him. He swam swiftly and went under its tail. He was in the middle of the lake, and the giant fish was ready to pounce again on him as he tried to move towards the ground, but the giant fish was fast, and this time, it swallowed Abhay.

Vayu, alone in the unknown forest, watched Abhay being swallowed by a giant black fish. It was confused by the sudden attack in water and the swallowing of Abhay. Since it was a celestial horse attached to Abhay, it decided to call for help. It grunted loudly and ran towards Kumeru.

Abhay found himself in the dark and was standing on its rough tongue. The fish had razor-sharp teeth all around the tongue, which Abhay was trying to avoid. It was difficult to stand on its tongue as the tongue was pushing him towards its teeth. Suddenly, the fish swallowed lots of water, and its mouth was flooded. Trying to find his balance on its tongue, he jumped out of the fish's tongue and broke through its skull. He landed on the fish's back and saw the lake water slowly turn red. The fish was dead with a broken skull, floating in the lake. He decided to swim back to the ground. Maybe enough swimming for today.

Abhay came out of the water and looked around for Vayu. Not finding Vayu, he thought that while grazing, it must have gone deeper into the forest. Abhay's voice echoed through the dense forest as he shouted Vayu's name, the sound bouncing off the trees and fading into the distance. He called out again, louder this time, but the silence that followed was unsettling. He decided to wait for Vayu to come back by himself and sat on the rock near the lake. His thoughts returned to the giant black fish. He thought,

"Whenever I come out into this forest from Kumeru, strange animals attack me. This forest seems to be full of such strange animals. How do they know that I am here?"

He had a long, tiring day, so he decided to lie down on the large rock near the stream until Vayu heard the same female voice, "Abhay, are you ok?"

He didn't know how to respond to that female voice. She seemed to know everything happening around Abhay, so many unknown secrets in his life.

He saw that he was lying under a mango tree, and it was loaded with ripe, yellow mangoes. He felt a pinch of hunger in his empty stomach. He climbed and plucked a few mangoes. Sitting on the rock, he started devouring those sweet mangoes. After his stomach was full, he lay on the rock to take a nap. He knew that Vayu would be back soon.

Pondering over the day's incidents, he heard footsteps of horses and other animals running towards his direction. He drew out his bow and arrow and pointed the arrow towards the incoming footsteps. Out of the clearing in the forest, he saw Virupaya and dozens of his soldiers walking towards him. Excitedly, Virupaya ran towards Abhay, hugging him, and said, "I had firm belief that nothing could have happened to you. Truth be told, I was not at all worried when we saw Vayu coming back without you." Chuckling, Virupaya said, "Looks like all disciples of Nansuki in Mahi are longing to meet Yamraaj[4]. Like ants to honey, they are all attracted towards you." Abhay smiled and hugged Virupaya.

Virupaya had realised that the forests around Kumeru were becoming dangerous. Since Nansuki knew about

---

4   Yamraaj – Lord of Death

Abhay's presence in Mahi, he was sending his disciples to attack Abhay. It was also dangerous for his tribe to venture outside Kumeru. He made a mental note to inform everyone not to venture out in the forests without his permission.

He didn't have to worry too much about Abhay's safety as he was fully capable of defending himself. Maybe he is a threat to Nansuki's followers. He smiled while thinking.

They were coming closer to the mountain, and he had to be prepared for any eventuality. He had to stock up on various herbs to strengthen the ape bodies and for healing battle wounds. Although the mountain had places where these herbs grew, there was a special place in the forest where more potent herbs grew in the wild.

There was a cave near the stream at the foothills where various potent herbs grew wildly. He hadn't gone there in a long time as the war threats were very few. There was no need to stock up on the herbs.

Virupaya ordered his troops to follow him into that cave and instructed them to pluck the blue-leaved herb. It was a potent herb that increased body strength and aided in healing battle wounds and cuts.

The cave was well hidden from anyone approaching the stream. If you didn't know about the cave, it was impossible to locate from the stream. It had a small entrance, and after walking a narrow path for a few metres, it opened into a very large hall. The hall was filled with all kinds of plants, some with medicinal properties and some poisonous. Only a trained eye could differentiate between poisonous and medicinal plants.

Virupaya, trained in ayurvedic [5]practice, had the ability to differentiate between them. He explained it to his crew, and they started looking for medicinal plants in the cave. Abhay, sitting on a large stone, looked at a bright green-coloured plant growing on the walls of the cave. Those plants were loaded with pink-coloured berries, which looked very delicious. He stood up and walked towards the nearest wall and plucked one berry. He was about to put that in his mouth when suddenly Virupaya's strong hand snatched it from his mouth and threw it on the ground.

Abhay, surprised by Virupaya's action, asked, "What happened? Why did you snatch the berry from my hand?"

Virupaya replied, "The forest is full of delicious and nutritious fruits. In the shadow of these fruits, there are also poisonous fruits. If you had taken one bite of that fruit, it would have caused your heart rate to beat faster and faster. In a few minutes, your heart would have exploded, and you would have died a painful death. All food is poison. Some kill faster than others."

---

5   Ayurveda – Indian Traditional Medicines

Abhay nodded in agreement and, chucklingly, said, "You are much smarter than your looks."

"It's opposite with you," immediately Virupaya replied.

Both laughed heartily and proceeded to leave the cave and head towards home.

Virupaya ordered his crew to deliver the herbs to the village ayurvedic doctor. He and Abhay decided to meet Ramdas and apprise him of the attack in the forest.

Ramdas was in discussion with his assistants when he saw them coming from the forest. Standing up, he walked up to Abhay and Virupaya and asked, "I hope everything is fine with you. I was not expecting you at this hour."

Virupaya replied, "Yes, everything is fine as long as Abhay is on our side."

He explained everything that happened in the forest.

Ramdas said, "It's good that you have brought the herbs as it will help us in case we are unable to reach the cave during the war."

Both nodded that it was prudent to be cautious in the coming days, as the war was just around the corner.

How and when, they were not sure of.

＜ - 5 - ＞

Prithvi and Mahi

Prithvi and Mahi are two different worlds connected through celestial energies, supporting each other. Whatever happens in one world, it is shared with the other world. If there are storms in one world, they create storms in the other world. Similarly, if there is famine on Prithvi, then famines are observed in Mahi. It's like two different worlds connected through an umbilical cord, constantly sharing energy with one another. At the minutest level, all is energy and energy is converted to matter. Both planets are in different dimensions but depend on each other to survive. If one dies, the other will not survive.

With such deep connections, the ability to control one world will give power over both worlds. Ancient rishis were able to decipher their connections and had developed powers to travel into both worlds with secret mantras. Those mantras were passed only to chosen disciples whose birth dates were chosen by the movement of constellations. All of them were overseen by three Great Rishis: Anesh, Medha, and Shaurya.

They were not present in physical form but manifested themselves in physical forms when they foresaw any danger to these worlds.

Over the millennia, various evil powers tried to control these different worlds, but they were subjugated by the three Great Rishis, except Nansuki.

Abhay, lying on his grass bed, was unable to sleep. He kept on hearing her calling his name. He had no idea who she was and why he felt such a strong, lifelong longing for her. He decided to take a walk in the jungle to clear his thoughts. So much was happening in his life that he was unable to think straight. He decided to take a swim in the lake behind the Lord Shiva temple.

After swimming for an hour, he lay on the grass and started singing softly. He had a melodious voice, and he found the atmosphere very relaxing.

Not finding Abhay in his hut in the morning, one of Virupaya's assistants woke him early morning and told him that Abhay was not in his hut. Someone had seen him going into the forest in the night. Alarmed, Virupaya woke up and summoned his crew. They were ready in no time and started to march towards the forest. Walking near the lake, they heard someone singing romantic songs.

Virupaya and his army were relieved and happy to see Abhay singing. Lying on the forest bed without any worries, Abhay was singing a melodious tune, a lover's longing for his lost lover. It lifted everyone's mood. From an anxious crew running towards the forest, suddenly everyone's mood changed, and they felt romantic. Everyone started dancing and singing together. They sat around and sang romantic songs one by one. It was a kind of celebration for them. Abhay was not only providing hope but also lifting their romantic spirits.

The sun was about to rise in the morning. Virupaya, in a cheerful mood, said, "Abhay, you sing so well with such a melodious voice. After you defeat Nansuki, you can start your singing troupe. You will become a famous singer."

Saying this, he started laughing loudly.

Abhay, looking at Virupaya with a smirk, replied, "I have already found the best dancer for the troupe."

Everyone laughed heartily over their banter. It was a very playful atmosphere. They were always trying to pull each other whenever they got a chance, like real siblings. They had the same love and attachment for each other, like siblings.

They decided to meet Ramdas before going home. When they were near the temple, they saw Ramdas finishing his yagna and ran excitedly towards them.

"With Lord Shiva's blessings, we have successfully completed our yagna and obtained the celestial bow, arrow, and quiver for Abhay. Its arrows have the power to ignite fiery arrows that can burn anyone. It is one of the most powerful celestial weapons in our world. It can also travel long distances," remarked Ramdas.

Excitedly, Ramdas performed the fire rituals before offering the weapon to Abhay. Everyone's faces lit up with joy, happiness, and confidence. Since it was granted by Lord Shiva, everyone decided to name it 'Pinaki'[6].

Everyone in the village was eagerly waiting for Abhay to come back. They had heard that Abhay left in the night and was seen walking towards the forest. They were all worried, but when they saw him returning with Virupaya, who was singing joyfully, they ran towards him. The village children crowded around, tugging at him eagerly. "Please, tell us what happened in the forest today!" they begged. "Why did you go there at night? How many monsters did you kill?"

Abhay cheerfully replied, "Nothing happened today. It was a boring day. I went to the forest just for a walk. No one came and disturbed me today."

Disappointed children shouted, "No, you are not telling us the truth. Please tell us today's adventures."

Making frightening faces, Abhay replied, "If I tell you, you all will get scared. I don't want to scare you. You will cry the whole night and will not be able to sleep

---

6   Lord Shiva's bow.

at night. Your mothers will blame me that I scared you and you couldn't sleep at night."

Children started jumping with excitement and replied, "We promise that we will not get scared and will sleep on time. We will also obey our mothers if you tell us today's story."

Standing straight, Abhay said, "If you promise me that you will not get scared, sleep on time, and obey your parents, then only I will tell you what happened in the forest."

"Yes, we all promise. Now tell us," all children shouted.

When Abhay started telling the incident while swimming in the stream, all village apes came and sat around Abhay. Everyone heard about his encounters in the forest and how he killed the giant fish in the stream. It was an awe-inspiring, unheard-of incident in their life. Their love, respect, and devotion towards Abhay increased manifold and believed that their days of living in fear are finally over.

Virupaya and Abhay sat in the hut discussing the happiness of their village. Abhay picked up the fruit basket, and both started to eat as they hadn't eaten anything since yesterday.

Resting on the bed, Abhay closed his eyes. She was standing in front of a temple, clad in a red saree[7], with

---

7   Traditional Indian dress.

long black hair flowing on her shoulders, a beautiful innocent face, and eyes full of longing for Abhay. Abhay's heartbeat started drumming up as he tried to come closer and touch her, but as he approached, she vanished, calling Abhay's name, her voice a haunting whisper carried by the wind. Abhay woke up with a racing heart, thinking about her and couldn't sleep any longer.

Who is she?
Who could tell him about her?
Why is there so much longing for her, and perhaps she is also missing him.
Is she real?
Where is she living?

Abhay kept on thinking about her and then slept.

Following day, Virupaya watched Abhay training in the ground and observed that Abhay was able to hit the moving target with ease. Abhay could also hit the target while riding Vayu. Satisfied with his performance, he thought to himself that Abhay's training under him was almost over. He looked up and prayed to Lord Shiva to give him direction for the next steps but dreaded the moment when Abhay would face Nansuki. Virupaya sensed that Nansuki knows about Abhay's presence and will be plotting to attack Abhay.

When and how was a dreadful moment. He knew about Abhay's powers, but Nansuki was one of the most powerful adversaries who was capable of defeating even the three Great Rishis. The very thought of Abhay facing Nansuki shuddered him.

While going back, they decided to meet priest Ramdas in the temple. It was their daily ritual to meet the priest before going back home. Ramdas was very wise and would tell them stories filled with wisdom.

Ramdas was waiting for them when they reached the temple. In an unnerving voice, he said, "Dear Abhay, can I ask you a small favour?"

"Sure, please go on," replied Abhay, surprised by the sudden request by Ramdas.

Ramdas, looking a little worried, said, "My brother, who is a priest in a village in Prithvi, just visited me. Their village is under the terror of an unusually dangerous bear. He told me that the villagers are afraid to go to their fields and even step out of their houses. It attacks unsuspecting people and eats them. It hides behind bushes and trees. The bear is especially fond of killing women and children. The whole village is living in an atmosphere of terror. Children and women have stopped coming out of their homes."

Abhay, calmly but with anger building inside, said, "If you can take me to their village on Prithvi, I will surely get the village rid of that bear."

Joyfully Ramdas replied, "Thanks a lot, Abhay. I knew that you wouldn't refuse to help hapless villagers."

Looking at Virupaya, Ramdas continued, "I will take only Abhay because the villagers might get scared of you. The apes on Prithvi don't live closely with humans. They have never seen an ape speaking human language."

Virupaya chuckled and said, "Abhay is more than capable of fighting any bear, big or small. I am not at all worried about Abhay."

Ramdas whispered a small mantra, and a magical portal opened in front of them to take them to Prithvi. Both walked inside and reached a village called Ramgarh on Prithvi.

Ramgarh was on the southern side of the continent, adjacent to the ocean. There were lush green forests on the mountainous region of the village. The people lived a rural lifestyle based on agriculture, fishing, and animal husbandry. They lived a harmonious lifestyle based on mutual respect and interdependence.

When they reached Ramgarh, Shantidas, Ramdas' brother, received them with folded hands and said,

"You are welcome in Ramgarh. We are very grateful for you to come to our village,"

Abhay smiled and said, "Please don't be so formal. Priest Ramdas' brother is like a brother to me. This is our responsibility. We are happy to help you and get rid of that bear's menace from this village."

"Please come with me. I will introduce you to our village head, Shyam Lal," Shantidas said. With grateful eyes, he motioned for them to follow him.

They walked towards the village and found the village head, Shyam Lal, sitting outside his house with a few other villagers. It was a normal practice for villagers to meet the village head outside his house regularly.

Shyam Lal stood up when he saw the village priest coming towards him. Coming closer, Shantidas said, "This is my brother Ramdas, who is also a priest in a Shiva temple. He is very wise and attained education from well-known rishis while travelling all over the world. He has brought his friend Abhay to save us from the bear's terror. Abhay is a very courageous warrior and graciously agreed to help our village."

Shyam Lal stood up and with folded hands, said, "We are very grateful for you coming to our small village. As the village head, it's my responsibility to save villagers from such animals. But in my whole life, I have never seen such a large bear that has an appetite for humans. Whenever we have tried to attack it with our spears, it doesn't seem to get hurt at all. It runs and hides in the forest. We hired an archer to hunt him last month. He went behind him and never came back. We fear that he might be killed by the bear in the forest."

With a frown, Abhay said, "Sounds strange, but don't worry, we will set up a trap for him tonight and get rid of that bear."

With tears in his eyes, Shyam Lal said, "I hope we get rid of that bear's terror soon. Everyone in the village is scared to go to their fields. If we don't get rid of that bear soon, then we will die of hunger. Without working in our fields, how will we feed our children."

Looking at the moist eyes of Shyam Lal, Abhay said, "Don't worry. We will take care of the bear. Until you are safe from its terror, we will not leave your village."

Happily satisfied, Shyam Lal invited them to his house for dinner as a token of gratitude. He extended the invitation to other villagers to join them.

They had built a community kitchen in the middle of the village, and everyone brought vegetables and fruits. The village women cooked various types of vegetarian dishes for the guests and were served food very respectfully. Abhay enjoyed all the tasty dishes and told Shyam Lal, "The food is really very tasty, and my stomach is full, but my heart is still craving for more."

Smiling Ramdas said, "Eat with your heart, and take some rest before we hunt the bear."

Touching his bloated stomach, Abhay said, "True, Ramdas, I will need rest to digest all the food I am galloping down my throat."

Both laughed heartily.

After dinner, Shyam Lal had arranged a small traditional singing and dancing ceremony for their guests. First, village children performed their dances, and then a young man and woman performed their traditional dance. It was a mesmerising performance, and Abhay enjoyed it very much.

When it got dark, everyone decided to go back to their houses to retire for the night.

While walking back to Shantidas' house, Abhay observed that the village was very quiet, and nobody was outside their homes. It looked like a curfew, with everyone hiding inside their homes.

He mentally noted and decided to leave for the bear hunt in a few hours after taking some rest. He had slept for only a few hours when he heard a shriek of a woman. He immediately woke up and found Ramdas and Shantidas standing near him.

Standing up from his bed, Abhay, anger in his eyes, said, "It's time to go hunt the bear and end his reign of terror."

"Right, we will both come with you."

"Don't worry, I will take care of that bear myself. You need not put yourself in any danger,"

"You are our guest, and we will not let you go alone."

"Okay. Come, but stay beside me all the time," Abhay replied when he saw the eagerness in both brothers' eyes.

Both brothers agreed and started running behind Abhay towards the noise. On the way, Shyam Lal, with his two villager guards with long spears, joined them.

Joining Abhay in the bear hunt, Shyam Lal said, "We will accompany you, and today we will finish the bear."

They started running quietly towards the shriek. Just outside the clearing, they saw a very large black bear walking towards the jungle. It carried a village woman over its shoulders. She was unconscious, likely from the shock.

Without any warning, one of the village guards threw his spear towards the bear. The spear struck the bear's shoulders and fell without harming it in any way. The bear looked back with angry, red eyes, dropped the woman on the ground, and growled loudly. It picked up the spear, broke it into two pieces, and growled louder.

Terrified, village guards took a few steps back, ready to run back to the village. The angry bear started running towards them furiously. Fearing a bear attack, everyone stepped a few steps back behind Abhay. Abhay stood his ground, and as the bear jumped on Abhay, he sidestepped from the bear's jump and kicked its stomach. The bear fell a few metres away. Angered, it charged again towards Abhay. As soon as it jumped, Abhay's fist collided with the bear's snout with powerful force, the impact reverberating up his arm. The bear's head snapped back, and with a low, guttural groan, it lost its balance. The immense weight of the creature shifted as it staggered, its paws scrambling for a moment before it tumbled backward. The ground seemed to shake as the bear crashed down, its massive body thudding against the earth. Dust and leaves flew up around it, settling slowly as the bear lay still, its chest heaving once before falling silent. The forest, which had been filled with the sounds of their struggle, grew eerily quiet as the bear stopped moving.

Abhay looked back at the villagers and asked,

"Are you all okay?"

"Yes, we are fine. Are you hurt?" everyone shouted.

"No, I am fine."

Abhay had his back to the bear and was talking with the villagers. He saw the terror in the villagers' eyes and found himself in the bear's grip on his neck. The bear had quietly stood up, come behind Abhay, and held him by his neck. The village guards, in fear, threw their spears and ran back to the village, the terror writ large on their faces.

Bear growled and said, "My Lord will be happy when I tear your head from your body." Surprised by the talking bear, Ramdas and Shyamdas' mouths stayed open.

Abhay pulled his body up in the air and forcefully kicked it in the stomach. The bear growled with pain and fell on its back, leaving Abhay free from his grip.

Abhay looked at the bear with anger and asked him,

"Who is your lord?"

"Who has sent you?"

Bear lying on his back replied, "Do you know who sent me? My Lord knew that you would come to save this village. I was waiting for you."

Saying this, the bear closed its eyes, muttered something, and a fireball appeared in his hands. Looking at Abhay, he threw it towards him. Shantidas jumped in front of that fireball and instantly burned.

Abhay, in anger, jumped on the bear and punched him hard on his face. He punched it harder and harder.

After some time, the bear closed its eyes and, while dying, said, "Lord will avenge my death. Your death is in his hands."

It fell on its back and died.

Abhay stood and came near Ramdas. Looking back, they saw a bear burned by some magic force, and only its ashes were in its place. Ramdas looked to where his brother had died a few seconds earlier. His ashes were lying there. Ramdas came closer and started crying, blaming himself for his death.

Abhay came near and placed his hand on his shoulder and said, "Your brother was very brave, and he sacrificed himself to save my life."

Ramdas nodded and cried loudly.

Both hugged and cried.

The woman was found unharmed but in shock. She was taken to the village doctor for treatment. There was a sense of happiness and sadness in the village.

They lost both their priest and enemy on the same day.

6

Shakti

During creation, the Universe created everything in pairs: male and female. For every object, to complete it, there was equal and opposite energy. Male and female energy joined, forming formidable energies. Over time, the separated male and female energies also broke down into multiple parts due to the degradation of their energies. There were only a few individual objects that carried pure male and female energies. Those separate and complete male and female energies were called divine beings. Very rare to find such beings.

On Prithvi, King Devraj was a pious and kind benefactor of rishis. His kingdom, Swarnabhumi, was one of the largest kingdoms in the world. Due to his pious nature, the three Great Rishis helped build a sprawling Shiva temple in his kingdom. He also built a sprawling university near the temple. People from all over the world would come to study ancient religious scriptures and learn astronomy, geometry, astrology, science, history, economics, and arts. The university was equipped with the latest tools, equipment, a library, and a hostel for thousands of students. Only the brightest students were accepted at the Lord Mahadev University in King Devraj's kingdom.

Rishis and learned scholars from around the world aspired to teach in the university. The teachers in the university were paid handsomely, and they were encouraged to work on independent research in their areas. Motivated teachers and the best talented students made the university a shining example of independent thinkers.

Lord Mahadev University was in the southern part of the city. It was spread over ten thousand acres. In the centre of the university, Lord Shiva's huge stone temple was built. It was the tallest structure in the university. All classrooms were built around the temple, divided into multiple parts. The laboratories were spread outside the classrooms, covering a large area. After laboratories, double-storied student hostels formed. The nutritious food was prepared by the university for all students. The sport academies were built just outside the students' hostel. Teachers and rishis lived just after the students' hostel. The teachers were given very beautifully built villas and apartments. The size of their housing depended on their seniority. There were multiple grocery stores in the university, spread around to minimise access to all inhabitants. There was a large-sized hospital built for thousands of inhabitants of the university. The outermost circle was occupied by the service staff of the university. The whole university was planned as a small self-governing city.

In the Shiva temple in the city, Yograj was the head priest. He had a small private residence adjacent to the temple where he lived with his wife, Yogini. Yograj was a disciple of the three Great Rishis and was always in touch with them.

A short while back, the three Great Rishis had brought a young girl to Yograj. Rishi Anesh said, "Dear Yograj, we would like to introduce Shakti to you. We would like her to stay with you as your daughter. Please keep her away from other people and don't let her go out from your private place. You shouldn't discuss her with anyone. At the right time, we will take her back with us."

Rishi Yograj and his wife, Yogini, lovingly looked at Shakti. Yogini walked towards Shakti and put her hands on Shakti's head and said, "We would be very grateful to keep her with us. You know that we don't have children. Shakti looks like our child, and we would keep her as our daughter."

Yograj looked happily at Shakti and continued, "You don't have to worry about her. She can stay with us as long as you want."

Rishi Anesh thanked both and quickly opened the magical portal, then went away. He looked in a hurry to leave.

The young girl started living with Yograj and his wife in the secluded garden in a small hut. The priest was aware of keeping her away from curious eyes. Her name was Shakti, and she was born from the three Great Rishis' yagna. Shakti and Abhay were born from the yagna to get rid of the world from Nansuki.

In the morning, walking towards Shakti's hut, they didn't find her there. She was fond of flowers and had planted many flower plants in the garden. She spent a lot of time tending to those plants.

They found Shakti in the garden corner where she was tending to her plants. They happily walked towards her, and Yograj said, "Dear Shakti, we are very fortunate to have you in our house. Rishi Medha has instructed us to inform you that all three Great Rishis will be visiting us today during our evening aarti[8]. They have told us that the time has come for you to be aware of your true self. You were born for a great purpose."

Yograj continued, "We request you to join us to fetch flowers from the garden near River Sarasvati. Today is a very special day for us, and for today's aarti, we want to pick the best flowers."

Shakti, joyfully walking towards them, said, "I would love to go near the river. I have seen a lot of beautiful flowers there."

---

8   Traditional Indian ceremony for Hindu God.

Saying this, Shakti lovingly hugged Yogini. Both Yograj and Yogini's eyes turned moist. Both had grown very fond of Shakti during her short stay with them. They got emotional after they felt that Shakti also felt the same. Since they were childless, they had grown fond of Shakti and started treating her as their daughter.

Shakti was of medium height with a dusky complexion. She had the most beautiful face one could ever see in their whole lifetime. Her eyes were as big as innocent deer eyes. She had a lean athletic body and was known to wake up early. She was born with the knowledge of various kinds of religious scriptures.

Walking on a small trail, three of them were briskly walking towards the flower garden, which was near the river. The garden had the best flowers in the whole city. They entered the garden and started picking up flowers. Shakti loved bright red roses and in search of them, came near the river bank. She saw beautiful red roses close to the flowing river and started picking them gently, unaware of the lurking danger in the river. This part of the river was infested with crocodiles, but they seldom ventured out into the open ground. With her back towards the river, she started looking for big red roses in the muddy area of the garden. The crocodiles silently surrounded her from all directions. Sensing some movement, Shakti stood up and saw that she was surrounded by crocodiles. They were not of average size but much larger than she had seen before. They surrounded her from all sides, and it was not possible to escape them on the ground. At any moment, they could attack her and drag her into the river.

Yogini, after filling her flower basket, was walking towards Shakti. From a distance, she saw Shakti was surrounded by crocodiles, ready to attack her anytime. Yogini screamed, and Yograj ran towards her. Both were shocked to see so many crocodiles surrounding Shakti.

Yograj observed that those crocodiles were in a kind of trance and were focused only on Shakti. He had never seen so many big crocodiles together in the same place. Crocodiles attacking anyone outside the waters was unheard of in the city. They were not from the river. Yograj started perspiring at the thought of meeting rishis without Shakti. He will lose his self-respect and purpose of life. He had kept Shakti like his real daughter, and if anything happens to her, he will not be able to live any longer.

One crocodile walked closer from behind to attack. Shakti skilfully jumped and landed on the crocodile's head. She stood on the head of the crocodile. It was trying to move away from her leg but couldn't move an inch. Its tail was moving ferociously as if its head was pinned to the ground.

Yograj and his wife came near the attack, and Yograj shouted, "Dear, jump on them and come here, out of reach of these crocodiles. They are looking very dangerous."

Astonishingly, both husband and wife saw Shakti smiling and rising a few metres up in the air, out of reach of any crocodile. Shakti was smiling, but her eyes were filled with fire. They had never seen anyone floating in the air, but Shakti was no ordinary girl.

Her fiery eyes started throwing fire towards crocodiles. The sudden fire attack from Shakti was unexpected, and the crocodiles started running away towards the river. Her fire attacks killed all of them instantly.

Perplexed, the husband-wife couple with open mouths stopped blinking. What they had just seen was some incident from fantasy storybooks, unheard of in real life: a flying girl killing menacing and dangerous crocodiles with fire in her eyes. They realised that they were in front of divinity and fell to their knees, tears flowing profusely from their eyes, unable to utter a word. Shakti slowly walked towards them and said, "Please stand up and treat me like your daughter. I am aware of who had sent them. They were not ordinary crocodiles."

Yograj and Yogini stood on their feet, hugged Shakti lovingly, and thanked their stars for bringing her into their life.

When the evening aarti started, Yograj observed that the three Great Rishis, Anesh, Medha, and Shaurya, were sitting near the havan[9]. He was excited to finish today's yagna and tell everything to the three Great Rishis about today's incident in the garden.

After finishing the yagna, Yograj went near the rishis and with tears in his eyes said, "We are very fortunate to meet you today and grateful for bringing Shakti into our life. We have witnessed a celestial event today in the flower garden. We can't tell you how fortunate we are to witness such an event."

Afterwards, he told the whole incident in the garden about Shakti and how she flew in the air and killed all the crocodiles with fire in her eyes.

All the rishis smiled, and Rishi Anesh said,

"Shakti is no ordinary girl. She was blessed by Lord Shiva and Goddess Parvati. She is a part of them and carries their energy with her. She is born for a great purpose, and we are here to take her with us so that she can be prepared for the coming great war and save both worlds."

Overhearing the imminent separation from Shakti, Yogini silently started crying and held Yograj's hand. Yogaraj tried to console her but couldn't stop his own tears. Over the last few weeks, both had become very fond of Shakti. They were childless and spent their whole life in the service of the Lord Shiva temple. After

---

9   Hindu fire ritual.

spending time with Shakti like their own daughter, it was difficult for them to let her go away. The pain of separation was unbearable for them.

Looking at their tearful faces, Shakti said, "I am not going away for forever, but will keep on visiting here. I have known you as my parents, and my respect and love will never diminish. Please bless me and let me go happily to fulfil my destiny."

Folding her palms in namaste, Shakti went to the three Great Rishis. "I believe the time has come for me to go with you and start preparing for the coming war," remarked Shakti. All rishis nodded, and Rishi Shaurya said a silent prayer. A portal opened in front of them. They all blessed the priest couple and walked straight into the portal.

Sumeru mountain was the tallest mountain on Prithvi, and humans were not able to climb it due to its extreme weather conditions, low oxygen levels, and steep height. The three Great Rishis had built their ashram near the top of the mountain in one of the caves. The cave was very large and had a pleasant weather, unlike the cold environment outside. It had multiple rooms, which were used when other rishis travelled to this cave. It was bright inside due to magically hanging lamps around the cave. The silent and serene environment inside was apt for long days of meditation. In the middle of the cave, a constant fire was burning in a rectangular-shaped area. It was also used for performing yagnas during astronomically significant days to please various gods for bringing peace and harmony in both worlds.

The three Great Rishis had performed austerity for hundreds of years and gained immeasurable powers from various deities. They could open portals to travel easily between different worlds and had vast knowledge of ancient scriptures and science.

After arriving in the cave, the rishis and Shakti sat around the rectangular fire. Shakti's face was brimming with serenity, even around the ancient rishis, as if she had prior knowledge of this meeting. Rishi Anesh explained to her about their daily routine, their cave, mountain Sumeru, and about themselves briefly. There was a calmness and maturity in their conversation. After Rishi Anesh finished explaining, Shakti calmly asked, "When will I meet Abhay? I think he is still not aware of me and his true purpose?"

"Abhay is in good hands in Mahi. Virupaya is a very noble soul, and he has trained Abhay well in archery and horse riding. Nansuki is still physically trapped in the prison, but he is able to mentally communicate with his followers. His followers have tried to attack Abhay, but he was able to conquer them all. He is slowly learning about his capabilities but still doesn't know about his true potential," remarked Rishi Shaurya.

"Nansuki is slowly gaining power, and he will be able to break free of his confinement very soon. We want both of you to be ready before he escapes so that you can get rid of our worlds from his terror forever. You stay with us until we train you to strengthen your mind to stop Nansuki controlling your mind. He is a master mind manipulator and can control multiple people's minds simultaneously. He is significantly weakened after the last war, but the current prison can't hold him for long. Before he acquires his full power, you both should be ready to fight with him."

"I am in your patronage and I am ready to be trained under your guidance."

After discussing for a few more hours, they decided to rest for the night and start the training from the next day.

Shakti's room was in one of the corners of the cave, a little hidden from the main hall. It was a small room with a bed and a study table in the corner. It was a comfortable room with basic amenities. The walls were made of stone but were warm to touch. The lamps were magically hanging in her room and could be turned off with thoughts.

It was all magical and ancient.

She sat down on the bed, thinking about the day and what lay ahead for her. She knew the deep connection with Abhay but didn't understand why Abhay doesn't understand that. Thinking about today's events, she slept soundly for the rest of the night.

In the morning, when she reached the main hall, she saw the rishis sitting around the fire meditating. She silently sat near them and started meditating. Rishi Shaurya asked her if she slept well, and she realised that they were communicating with her through mind, without speaking any words. Surprisingly, she could also communicate with her mind. She felt a deep connection with them. The rishis explained about the previous war when they had captured Nansuki and imprisoned him in the deep corners of Prithvi.

They knew that their powers would not be able to contain him for long in the prison. They performed a yagna to please Lord Shiva and Goddess Parvati for a long time. Pleased with the three Great Rishis, they were blessed with Abhay and Shakti. Nansuki's powers were increasing every day, and the rishis wanted to train them for the next war. The rishis wanted Shakti and Abhay to be ready before Nansuki breaks free from the prison.

The training schedule for Shakti was to meditate and strengthen her mind.

Mind is one of the most powerful tools in human's possession. All of the Universe can be created and destroyed from the mind. To achieve anything worthwhile in life, it is important to create it first in your mind. Once it is achieved in the mind, it finds a way to manifest in real life.

7

King Devraj

King Devraj was a kind and justice-loving king of Swarnabhumi, who cared for his subjects like his children. He had helped build the society based on meritocracy. He built residential schools in each district based on the concept of gurukuls[10], which were run by rishis. All children, irrespective of their parents' social standing, were admitted to their district schools. There were no school fees, but the rich were motivated to donate for various school activities, but outside their children's school district. This was done to avoid any kind of preferential treatment to children of the rich families. Social harmony was encouraged throughout the kingdom. The children wore the same dress, ate the same food, and stayed in the same simple hostels. They were educated in respect for others (extending to animals), ancient religious scriptures, history, mathematics, geography, civil rights, and a special focus on science. Independent thoughts were encouraged throughout the gurukuls.

---

10 Residential school during ancient India run by the Rishis.

Physical labour was not looked down upon in Swarnabhumi. In gurukuls, children were assigned physical jobs such as cleaning, gardening, and washing. Children also participated in various social initiatives in their towns, cultivating respect for physical work and for people involved in laborious tasks.

Swarnabhumi was located on the southern side of the longest range of mountains, where the three Great Rishis lived in their cave. It had the largest and strongest army on the continent, well-trained in all aspects of warfare. King Devraj had never attacked any other kingdom and always respected their neighbour's kingdom, no matter how small or big. Children's education and healthcare of their citizens were taken care of by the state. Farmers were protected and supported by various government schemes so that they were less dependent on nature's vagaries. They were paid on time with the right prices for their produce. Citizens were encouraged to work in those areas where they performed their best, whether it was artistic vocations, the study of religious scriptures, the army, the police, trading with other kingdoms, etc. All citizens were free to choose their profession without any restrictions.

Public administration held competitive exams in the kingdom for hiring in government departments. Nepotism was frowned upon and discouraged at all levels. There were harsh penalties for any corruption in the government administration.

There was freedom to choose your vocation, but strict adherence to rules and regulations was mandatory.

This freedom led to the prosperity of their kingdom. The best talent from the neighbouring kingdoms immigrated and set up their businesses. The law and order were strictly implemented. There were heavy fines for cheating, and contracts were legally enforced. It had an environment of security, and women were encouraged to work free from any limitations.

King Devraj had two sons, twins. During their birth, there were medical complications that led to their impaired cognitive abilities. The king announced that he would choose the heir based on the person's capabilities and not on their birth. It was an unheard-of decision in the history of their kingdom.

The people of Swarnabhumi loved and respected their king.

The Gurukul of Ashok Nagar had planned an annual weeklong stay in a nearby forest, Dandkund. The Ashok Nagar region fell in the northern upper mountainous part of the kingdom. Dandkund forest received continuous rainfall all year round. The forest was full of a variety of herbs, plants, insects, birds, and animals. Its lush greenery was abundant with fruits and wild vegetables. The forest resort for children was barricaded from all sides for their safety from wild animals. The gurukul administration had built various play areas for a physical strength training regimen for students. Children used to love coming to the forest resort and staying in the wild environment.

The resort was in the middle of the forest. Various streams and lakes were nearby. The children's cottages were in the middle of the resort, and various physical strength training equipment was also located near the children's living area. The teachers' and trainers' cottages surrounded the children's cottages. The outermost cottages were occupied by guards and support staff. The resort was designed for children's security. Ample care was taken during the children's movement in the forest area during their outside training.

On this trip, Rishi Mander was heading the forest expedition. He was known as a very kind but strict administrator. He didn't like anyone breaking the rules, which he believed helps to build children's character. He had planned the whole expedition well in advance and scheduled every hour of the day.

They had reached here on horse carriages, and all students were allocated cottages. The younger students had the cottages inside the resort, then older students, and then by teachers. The resort was secured by professional soldiers who were trained to minimise the animal-man conflict. They were also fully aware of the forest terrain and had a good understanding of wild animals, insects, reptiles, and herbs available in the forest.

On the first day in the Dandkund, it rained heavily, and children were not able to go out of their cottages. They spent their day playing indoor games and chatting the whole day. The second day was cloudy without rains. Rishi Mander decided to go out near the river and teach children about the herbs in that region. Rish Mander and his assistant teachers took children and showed them various herbs and their applications on the human body. The children were very impressed with those herbs as some of them had strong healing powers. Some herbs could join broken bones in a few hours; others could bring eyesight to blind people. After spending the whole day in the forest, they decided to go back to their resort and started collecting the material which they had brought with them.

A wild boar, sixty inches tall and weighing more than two hundred kg, was looking at the gathering from the other side of the river. It was much larger than the normal-sized wild boar and was unheard of to be this big. A few children spotted it and informed Rishi Mander. When Rishi Mander saw it, a chill went down his spine. He knew that a wild boar this size was unnatural, and it was a bad omen to be sighted. He immediately gave orders to the accompanying soldiers and teachers to take the children back to the resort. Once everything was packed, and they were starting to return, Rishi Mander looked back again in the boar's direction; it was gone. Not knowing whether to be relieved or scared, they returned briskly to their camp.

Coming back to the resort, he asked soldiers to close all gates properly and keep a strict vigil around the perimeter with all their weapons. Rishi Mander was worriedly walking inside his cottage and decided to inform King Devraj. He wrote a letter and asked his assistant to send it urgently through their delivery pigeons.

The fastest communication method in the kingdom was pigeons. All senior government officials carried their delivery pigeons to send urgent messages to their departments. This method allowed the central ministry to keep a close eye on all events in their kingdom. In the likely event of any pre-emptive measure requirement, suitable actions were taken by concerned central ministries.

Night was gloomy, and there were not many wild animal noises on that night. There was a palpable terror among all children and teachers, and all were speaking in hushed voices.

Rishi Mander decided to return to the gurukul and leave the forest in the early morning. He didn't want to take any risks with the children. He instructed his staff and soldiers to pack everything and leave in the morning.

They packed everything on their horse-drawn carriages and started their return journey early morning. It was a cloudy day, and the journey would take a day to reach their gurukul. They had to travel half a day in the forest, which made Rishi Mander very worried. After a few hours of travel, they decided to rest for some time and have lunch. Carefully, without making much noise, they started cooking lunch and instructed students to stay together and not wander around.

Their stop was near a small lake with crystal clear water. The area had a few fruit-bearing trees. A few of the Rishis' assistants were ordered to collect fruits for everyone but given the clear instruction not to wander far from their stop.

The accompanying cooks cooked delicious meals of a few vegetables, lentils, and boiled rice. Children were so tired from their journey that they finished their meals in no time. They were not only tired from their journey but also a little scared from last day's incident. They were excited for the stay in the forest, but the rare sighting of such a wild boar had made them scared. They always looked forward to their forest stays.

As soon as everyone finished their food, they heard some loud, high-pitched squealing. Everyone looked in the direction and saw the same wild boar standing and readying to charge towards the group. Rishi Mander asked the soldiers to attack and kill the boar and simultaneously asked his assistant to take all children in the carriages. Soon, all children were packed in the carriages, and the assistants started to steer away the carriages towards the town.

The wild boar had tracked them, which was not their normal behaviour. It was not even a normal-looking wild boar. Something was evil about that boar.

Wild boar came charging towards them, and soldiers started attacking it with their arrows. None of the arrows were successful in hurting the wild boar. While charging, it changed its direction and attacked the nearest soldier, killing him on the spot. It had a long horn on its head with sharp edges. It glided its sharp horn into the chest of the soldier. Soldiers were terrified of that animal as they didn't know how to kill such an animal. It was an unusual wild boar in every sense: ferocious, large, sword-like horn, and unnatural ability of tracking.

Everyone was terrified and thought that their end was coming today.

Boar looked at the rishi, Mander, and grunted loudly to charge towards him.

The boar was running ferociously towards the rishi. The rishi was terrified as none of the soldiers' arrows were able to hurt or stop it.

They heard a loud conch from behind. Probably, someone had heard their cries and came to help. They were surprised when they looked back.

King Devraj, on his celestial chariot, was coming towards them. Aiming from his large bow, he shot an arrow spewing fire and hit the wild boar in its heart, killing it instantly.

The ferocious, unkillable wild boar lay dead in front of their eyes.

Looking at the dead wild boar, there was a sense of relief on everyone's face. From facing near death a few seconds ago to total relief, Rishi Mander walked towards the king with folded hands in the form of namaste and said, "Blessed are the people of your kingdom. We thank you for your immediate response and for coming to save our lives. We are very grateful to you."

Stepping down from his chariot, King Devraj, looking worried, responded, "It is my duty to save my subjects. I have done nothing special. Children and Rishis are the future of our kingdom, and taking care of them is my first responsibility. I hope none of you are hurt."

King Devraj came closer to inspect the dead boar. Before him, it breathed its last breath and released a blue-coloured fume from its mouth. Afterwards, it started becoming smaller.

In front of the king lay the dead, normal-sized domestic pig.

The king and rishi were surprised to see such a transformation of the dead pig. By that time, the king's personal contingent also arrived and took charge of the situation. King Devraj ordered them to carry the pig's dead body to inspect it thoroughly for any anomalies. It was important to know its origins and its transformation.

King Devraj murmured, "Not a good omen. The three Great Rishis must be informed of this incident at once."

Worryingly over the incident, the king thought to himself, "I hope there will be no more war with the devils. Last time, thousands of my people lost their lives."

King Devraj told the rishi that the children and his other teaching staff have already been escorted by his contingent and they will reach safely in Ashok Nagar Gurukul. Considering today's situation, he has also deployed more soldiers around the gurukuls in the kingdom.

While going back, both agreed that it was none other than Nansuki who was responsible for today's mayhem.

He mentally took a note to inform the great three Rishis about today's incident as soon as he reached the city.

Prime Minister Keshav and Defence Minister Raghupati were seated in the king's court with King Devraj.

Prime Minister Keshav said, "This is a very unfortunate and worrisome event. We received reports from the other side of Dandkund that villages were ransacked and looted. We had believed that it could be marauding small tribes from across the border. Today's incidents prove that it could be more sinister than imagined. We need to be alert to any such incident in other areas."

Defence Minister Raghupati, impatiently with closed fists, replied, "I agree with you, Keshav. Before the situation gets out of control, we need to keep extra vigil. I will increase the reinforcements in the border areas and will send a team to investigate in the forest."

Listening silently to both of his closest ministers, Devraj remarked, "It was not an ordinary pig, but I believe it was infused with some black magic. We need to be very careful while inspecting the forest. I don't want to lose any of my soldiers. Please take care that the soldiers are sent into the forest only to report back, and under no circumstances should they engage with the enemy. Keshav, please inform the three Great Rishis of today's incident."

Both nodded and left the court immediately.

– 8 –

Dandkund

Later in the king's court, Rishi Mander was sitting next to the king, and his cabinet ministers were sitting on both sides of the table. Rishi Mander said, "Thanks for saving our lives today in the forest. We are very grateful to you. I have been taking students to the forest for the past twenty-five years, and I have never faced this kind of danger. That was no ordinary boar but was enhanced by some kind of black magic. I believe Nansuki's disciples are building a sanctuary in that place. That boar was some kind of guard of that sanctuary. I had a glimpse of some movement around that area. Building a secret haven in the forest can mean only one thing: there are some sinister activities going on there. I urge you to take it very seriously and send your best platoon to investigate the area."

King Devraj nodded and looked at his ministers. They were all looking worried after hearing Rishi Mander's statements.

Keshav, Prime Minister of Swarnabhumi, came from a very humble background but had a sharp analytical mind. He was short but had big, discerning eyes. It was rumoured that he could read anyone's mind while listening. He spoke softly and gave so much confidence to his listener that others would invariably tell him all their secrets. He was well-read and was known to analyse every small detail before taking any decision. King Devraj trusted Keshav's instincts and never took any decision without first discussing with him.

King looked at Keshav and asked, "Did you get any prior information about Dandkund, or is it the first reported incident?"

With a straight face, Keshav replied, "This is the first time we have received any such reports. Maybe they have just arrived in the forest to build something. I haven't received any news of the building of any camp in Dandkund."

"Could we have missed any information?" asked Devraj with a frown.

Keshav replied in a thoughtful manner, "Possible. Dandkund is a dense forest and covers a very large area of our kingdom. It also shares a boundary with a few of our neighbouring kingdoms. It's not practical to guard the whole forest as it will drain our limited resources. Without any proof, we can't even discuss it with our neighbours. Based on Rishi Mander's suspicions, we have already sent one of our battalions to investigate the area and report any illegal developments."

King Devraj nodded and looked at his Defence Minister, Raghupati.

Defence Minister Raghupati was a tall, well-built, and fearsome man. He was known to charge from the front and had built a well-trained and disciplined army. Raghupati had a lot of interest in the newer warfare technologies and built a separate division of weapon specialist scientists. That scientific division's only focus was research and development of technological advancement of weapons, soldiers' dietary needs, and training. He was single-handedly responsible for Swarnabhumi army's technological superiority in the whole world.

Raghupati, observing concern on King Devraj's face, nodded and said, "I have sent my best team to investigate the area. We will capture all criminals if they are operating in Dandkund with any ill will towards our kingdom."

King Devraj replied immediately with a stern look, "Don't engage with the enemy. Scan the area and send us the report. Based on the threat, we will act. I don't want to put our soldiers in any unnecessary danger. If the enemy has built a military camp in the forest, then our soldiers might endanger their lives if they engage with them."

"Yes, my king. We will do as you order," replied Raghupati cautiously.

Concluding the gathering, Kind Devraj looked at Rishi Mander and said, "My guards will drop you back to your gurukul, and you have nothing to worry about. With Lord Shiva's blessings, we will investigate and clear the forest of any criminal activities. I hope that it was one kind of stray incident. We will thoroughly investigate the area. If any action is required, we will take strict action and remove it from the forest."

After Rishi Mander and Raghupati left the King's chambers, the king worriedly looked at Keshav and remarked, "If Rishi Mander's suspicions are correct, then we should inform the three Great Rishis. If Nansuki's disciples are involved, it might be dangerous to send our soldiers to fight."

"You are right. I will right away get the golden ashes and send the message to the great three Rishis. If Nansuki's followers are building a military camp so near our kingdom, the target could be only our beloved Swarnabhumi. If we are attacked by them, then we would be ill-prepared to defend our kingdom. Rishi Mitra is known to attack ferociously. He doesn't follow the normal rules of war, and he might use black magic or unholy alliances. We need to be prepared as he can launch an attack without any warning."

"This is much more serious than previously thought," the worried king remarked.

The three Great Rishis had instructed all Kings to inform them if they had any suspicion of Nansuki's involvement in their kingdoms. All Kings were provided with golden ash to be poured onto burning wood. The golden ash had magical power to be visible in the rishi's cave on Sumeru. As soon as they were burned, their image was reflected in the rishi's cave in Sumeru. This was the fastest way to send a message to the three Great Rishis. The three Great Rishis always visited the kingdom where the golden ashes were burned. In the current climate, the rishis were alert in investigating the incidents related to Nansuki. They never hesitated to visit the kingdom.

After pouring golden ash on the burning wood in the king's chamber, Keshav hurriedly came back and stood beside the king, waiting for the great three rishis. A few minutes later, a portal opened in front of their eyes, and Rishi Medha walked in from the portal.

Both Devraj and Keshav touched the rishi's feet with respect. King Devraj said, "Respected rishi, we encountered a strange incident in the forest today. We thought it would be better if we could inform you about it. The head of Ashok Nagar Gurukul, Rishi Mander, had taken students to Dandkund forest for their regular educational trip. In the forest, they encountered an unusually large wild boar. Our soldiers' arrows were unable to hurt it. I had to use a celestial arrow to kill it. When it died, it turned into a normal-sized domestic pig. Before I could kill it, it managed to kill a few of our soldiers. Rishi Mander suspects that it was some kind of guard of a secret place. There is only one person who can build such a secret camp in a remote location."

Rishi Medha thought for a few seconds and asked, "What was unusual about the wild boar?"

"What do you mean?"

"Apart from the large size, is there anything else you want to tell me?"

"Yes, it had a razor-sharp thorn on its head, and it tracked rishi's team from the forest. A boar tracking someone over a day is unheard of in the forest."

"Anything else?"

"Yes, I forgot to mention that its size changed when it died, and it released a blue-coloured fume from its mouth before it died."

"That's what I wanted to check. It was infused with black magic, which is the expertise of Rishi Mitra. I believe the matter is very serious. Looks like Rishi Mitra is building a camp in Dandkund, hidden from all of us. Building a camp in the forest is an indication of preparations for an attack."

"How is it possible? Under our very nose. That's reckless,"

"Rishi Mitra is not reckless. He is an expert planner, and I believe that he is planning something against your kingdom. His camp would be a few hours away from your city."

"That's correct,"

"Anything is possible when Rishi Mitra is involved. I will go back and discuss it with my fellow Rishis. In case of any further instructions for you, we will come back and inform you."

Saying this, Rishi Medha opened the magical portal and walked back in, leaving the King's Chamber.

Rishi Medha narrated the incident to his fellow rishis in the presence of Shakti. Rishi Shaurya remarked, "Looks like Rishi Mitra has built his base in Dandkund forest. He must be trying to build an army of Nansuki's disciples hidden away in the forest. We can't give him enough time to gather more fighters and help Nansuki."

Looking into his fellow rishis' eyes, Anesh said, "Time has come to visit Abhay. We should plan to attack Rishi Mitra's camp in the forest before it's too late."

All rishis nodded in agreement. The war was coming sooner than later.

Shakti had been silently listening to their conversation with many questions running in her mind. She asked, "Should we travel to Mahi?"

All rishis nodded in unison, and Rishi Medha said, "We will leave early after our morning rituals. Tonight, we need to meditate and seek Lord Shiva's blessings. The next few days are going to be important for the wellbeing of our worlds. May the Lord bless us all in this endeavour."

Shakti came back to her room, and questions started popping up in her mind.

"Finally, I will meet Abhay."
"Will he recognise me?"
"What will I say to him?"
"Will he come back here?"
"I have to ask so many questions,"

Lying on her bed, she slept, with so many questions in her mind.

- 9 -

Abhay and Shakti

Abhay had a tiring day. He practised the whole day with his bow and arrow, riding Vayu. Vayu had become very close to Abhay, and they spent whole days together, either practising or riding all over the adjoining forests. He had become a skilled archer and could shoot moving targets while riding on Vayu.

One day, Abhay went to Virupaya's training camp where soldiers were being trained in various fighting techniques. Virupaya was a mature and competent leader; he was very skilled in selecting people according to their competencies. He was always observing the newly joined cadets and, based on their interests, he would assign them jobs in the army.

His training camps were well-organised into various smaller units. He believed in rewarding competent soldiers to give them leadership positions. He expected them to behave like a leader, and juniors to follow orders. Indiscipline in the army was not accepted. Soldiers were very loyal to Virupaya and always worked hard to please him, but he was a difficult leader to be pleased by small gestures.

"Do you think I can help you train your soldiers?" on the way back in the evening, Abhay asked Virupaya.

"What kind of training?" asked Virupaya, curtly.

"Probably archery or horse riding," replied Abhay with a frown.

With a smile, Virupaya asked, "But you yourself are learning. How can a trainee train others?"

Abhay, visibly irritated, said, "You know I am a good archer and ride well on Vayu."

"You have a celestial bow and arrow; it will reach its target even if you close your eyes. Similarly, your Vayu is also celestial," Smiling Virupaya replied.

Angrily, Abhay replied, "You think I can't target with an ordinary bow and arrow and ride an ordinary horse."

Virupaya chuckled and said, "I will be honoured if you also train our soldiers. They have a lot of respect for you, and I know that they would learn better from you."

Virupaya and Abhay were always pulling each other's legs and never left anything to chance. From the next day, Abhay joined Virupaya in his training camp, and they started spending most of their time together.

Alone, he always had a feeling of uneasiness, as if he was incomplete and was missing someone important in his life. He heard her voice all the time, without realising her identity. Virupaya was unhelpful in these pursuits as he was preparing for the coming war and had no time for romantic issues.

Evenings were spent playing with children in the village. The children were fond of him, and he was fond of them. He loved playing with them, hanging on trees, jumping from one branch to the other. When all got tired, he would tell them fictional monster stories of the forest. Everyone enjoyed Abhay's monster-beating stories.

Today, Abhay was telling them a story of a flying snake in the forest which had attacked Abhay while he was eating his lunch. All the children were listening to his story with apt attention. Abhay saw Virupaya and Ramdas coming towards him hurriedly. Virupaya came near Abhay and said, "We need to discuss something very important with you. Can you please come with us to your hut?"

"What happened? Is everything all right?" Abhay replied in a surprised tone.

Virupaya curtly replied, "Yes, everything is fine."

Abhay turned towards the children and said, "Please forgive me today. I will finish the story tomorrow and will also bring sweet berries from the forest beyond the river." Although unhappy, all children agreed, thinking about the sweet, mouthwatering berries.

Abhay climbed and reached his hut. Virupaya and Ramdas were already inside the hut, waiting for him.

As soon as Abhay entered, Ramdas said, "Apologise for troubling you at this hour, but it was an urgent matter that we wanted to discuss with you. Rishi Anesh mentally messaged me a few minutes back and told me that they would be coming in the morning to take you. They informed me that the time has come to work on your destiny. He didn't elaborate much, but I assume that some terrible war is starting soon. In that war, you must play an important role. Please wake up early in the morning and come to the temple. I know you have a lot of questions now, but it would be better if you could wait for one more day. I believe all your queries will be answered tomorrow."

Abhay thoughtfully replied, "Sure."

Virupaya and Ramdas went back, deep in their thoughts and a little worried about tomorrow. Abhay went back to the children and finished his story of flying snakes.

Abhay couldn't sleep and kept on thinking about the next day. The three Great Rishis are venerable rishis, and they have kept balance in both worlds with their foresightedness. The world owes a lot to them. Everyone has always spoken highly of them. It would be the first time he would be meeting them. He was a little nervous. Maybe his destiny was unfolding before him sooner than later. It must be something important that they all are visiting tomorrow to meet him.

"I hope I meet her soon?"

Thinking about tomorrow, he dozed off.

She was wearing a red saree, the most beautiful face in the world, long flowing dark hair over her shoulders, smiling, beckoning him, calling Abhay's name.

He woke up suddenly with a racing heartbeat. He couldn't sleep any longer that night. Just her image and her calling his name. He thought he had fallen madly in love with her and was unable to wait any longer to meet her. Her face, her voice, so much grace and love.

Was she an angel?

Abhay couldn't sleep much during the night. He was excited for tomorrow. He was about to meet the three Great Rishis, and his destiny might be revealed tomorrow. Maybe he is not as great as everyone believes him to be, maybe he turns out to be an ordinary person. Soon, he will know. The future will be revealed tomorrow.

He woke up early in the morning and reached the temple before Virupaya. Ramdas was already there, ready, waiting for both. Virupaya soon arrived after Abhay.

Abhay, Ramdas, and Virupaya were waiting in the temple when they saw the three rishis walk in through the portal. The portal was still open, and she walked in last. Abhay's heartbeats were racing as if he was running on a mountain. He was mesmerised by her beauty. Shakti was also looking at him. Their eyes met and locked on each other. Both stopped observing anything else except each other. They had seen and felt each other every moment of their life.

The three Great Rishis looked at them, smiled, and breaking their attention, coughed loudly. Rishi Anesh said, "You have a lifetime together. Bring your attention to the current crisis and spend eternity together."

Everyone lovingly smiled, looking at both.

Shakti and Abhay blushed and apologised for their conduct.

Abhay, Virupaya, and Ramdas welcomed and touched the rishis' feet and took their blessings.

The three Great Rishis looked alike. Maybe if you spend a lifetime together, your face also starts looking similar. Long white hair and flowing beard. The hairs were tightly tied together on their head. Two pieces of white cloth covering their lean bodies. Glowing faces with knowledge and wisdom. They had deep black eyes, eyes which can pierce into anyone's soul. All of them carried a wooden stick in their hands, but it was not for helping them to walk. Maybe it had a different function. They all had a perfectly fit body without any sign of any wrinkle. They were wearing rudraksha [11]beads on their neck, arms, and wrists.

Rishi Anesh softly said, "We are thankful to Virupaya and Ramdas for taking care of Abhay. We have observed Abhay's training from a distance and are very pleased with his progress. You have done a great service for both worlds."

Looking at Virupaya, he continued, "You must prepare your troops for the coming war. We can't let Nansuki's disciples become stronger. The war will invariably come to Mahi."

Finally, Rishi Anesh looked at Abhay and said, "I know you have a lot of questions about yourself. There was a reason we kept you away from Prithvi. We didn't want to take any risk on your life during your training. Enemies are looking for you everywhere. They have sensed your presence. Mount Kumeru was the safest place for you in both worlds. Both of you are Lord Shiva and Goddess Parvati's blessing. We welcome you to come with us and fulfil your destiny."

With folded hands, Abhay replied, "I am very grateful to you. I am ready to follow you. Please guide me to fulfil my destiny."

---

11 Rudraksha – rudraksha beads worn by traditional Hindu rishis, related to Lord Shiva.

Abhay excused himself to say goodbye to his close friends, Virupaya, and Ramdas.

Virupaya hugged Abhay tightly with moist eyes and said, "Life will not be the same without you. I wish I could follow you and never leave your side."

Abhay nodded in agreement with moist eyes and said, "The day is not far when we would be together. I know only you in my life as family. Our bond is stronger than brothers. Nothing is random in this world. We have been together for ages. I will be back as soon as possible."

Hugging Ramdas and thanking him for his support during his stay, Abhay quickly left them and walked behind the rishis in the portal.

Abhay saw that they walked in some kind of magical cave where the lamps were floating. A rectangular firepit with burning wood was in the middle, and the nice weather was filled with sandalwood aroma. It was an otherworldly place with a lot of pious energy. He felt relieved and at home.

Rishi Shaurya explained to him how they both were born from their yagna. Lord Shiva and Goddess Parvati blessed the rishis with Abhay and Shakti, pure souls capable of fighting Nansuki, the most powerful threat to both worlds.

He also explained the recent incident in Dandkund forest and their apprehensions about Rishi Mitra, a disciple of Nansuki, planning and encouraging Nansuki's disciples to attack both worlds.

Abhay heard everything and sat near the fire to contemplate his next steps. He closed his eyes and was surprised to hear Shakti's voice in his mind. Surprised, he opened his eyes and saw Shakti sitting in a meditative posture near him. He also closed his eyes and heard her speak again. He realised that they both had the power to communicate with one another through their minds. Everything was happening very fast and unprecedented in his life. He didn't realise his true powers, and mostly, he wasn't aware of them.

He wanted to spend time with Shakti, get to know her, and talk for hours with her, but destiny had other plans for him. He was supposed to fight Nansuki, an evil so powerful that even the three Great Rishis couldn't harm him. They had imprisoned him, but he could soon escape from there. Even while imprisoned, he could summon his disciples and trouble both worlds. He was not sure how he would be able to fight such a powerful devil.

Shakti said, "Don't worry, Abhay. I am with you and will help you bring peace in both worlds. Together, we are invincible, and no evil power can hurt us." Abhay, happy and relieved, replied, "I know, Shakti. We both are One, and it's our destiny to bring peace in both worlds. With you, I feel invincible."

They both looked into each other's eyes, smiled, and were happy to be together.

When they were alone, Shakti asked Abhay if he wanted to see where they were living on Sumeru. He nodded, and they decided to go out of the cave.

Before stepping out of the cave, they saw that it was frozen outside for miles. There was no soul, no vegetation around for miles. All they could see was ice all around, probably metres deep, covering mountains all around.

Looking at Abhay, Shakti said,

"I will create a magical, transparent bubble around us. The bubble will also keep us warm. It will fly, and I will show you around the mountain and nearby places."

"That will be so nice to look at, Prithvi. This is my first time here. I believe, after our birth, I was transported to Mahi."

"You had to spend some time in Mahi to meet Virupaya and his people. Both the worlds are our responsibility. I saw the love and devotion of Virupaya and Ramdas for you."

"They both are great people. I am glad I spent time with them. I have learned a lot from both."

Talking and laughing, they soared above the mountains. Abhay looked at the beautiful mountains and valleys. The stars were sparkling in the sky like diamonds. They were flying over the icy mountains and could see darkness below the mountainous region. Those were the plains where most of the people lived in a warmer climate.

Without realising, they spent the whole night flying over. When they realised it was early morning, they decided to come back to their cave.

Lying in their bed, they were both happy to be together.

– 10 –

Rishi Mitra

King Meghnath was a very religious king. He held regular discourses on religious scriptures and rewarded religious gatherings with luxurious food and gifts. He believed that such regular praise to gods in his kingdom would keep the gods happy. However, he lacked an understanding of the spiritual context behind religious scriptures. Behind all the celebrations was his insatiable attachment to power to acquire luxurious things in life. He had filled his cabinet mostly with yes men who agreed with the king on all matters.

This led to a general deterioration of law and order in his kingdom. The citizens' wellbeing was ignored, and there was high resentment against the king. Meghnath spent fortunes on religious gatherings but failed to provide better living conditions for its citizens.

The religious gathering of Meghnagar was joined by all rishis and religious leaders. It provided a religious environment for all of them. A few days of such festivities provided them with the opportunity to meet rishis from other kingdoms.

Rishi Shivam was also invited for the yagna.

Sitting in his gurukul, Rishi Shivam called his favourite students into his room. He was very proud of them. They performed well in all their exams, lived a very disciplined life, were very kind to their juniors, and always ready to go beyond their limits. He wanted to take them to the nearby kingdom, Meghnagar, for the religious event. The king had invited all rishis for the yagna, which was performed for the wellbeing of his kingdom's prosperity. Meghnagar was a day's journey away on foot from their gurukul. They had to pass through the forest for the journey. His favourite students, Anesh, Medha, Shaurya, and Mitra, walked into Rishi Shivam's cabin. Rishi Shivam happily said, "Welcome all. I am so happy to see your performance this year. All our teachers are very happy and proud of your performance."

Medha replied, "Respected rishi, we are thankful to you for providing us this opportunity. We all try to do our best."

Other students nodded in agreement.

The rishi continued, "There is a yagna being held in Meghnagar, and the king has invited me as the chief priest. This year, I would like you all to accompany me and meet rishis from different kingdoms. Your education in this gurukul is mostly complete. Your visit will help you in meeting other rishis of other kingdoms."

Shourya replied, "Thanks a lot for the opportunity. We are highly grateful to you."

Rishi Shivam lovingly looked at his favourite students and said, "You can go to your rooms. We will start tomorrow early morning."

In the morning, Rishi Shivam left with his four students for Meghnagar.

The atmosphere in Meghanagar was full of festivities. The king had taken care of visitors' accommodation in luxurious camps built for the event near the king's palace. There were priests from all the neighbouring kingdoms. The yagna was started at an auspicious time and was held for three days.

After the yagna, the king had planned religious sermons by a few rishis who spoke about the mythology behind the religious scriptures. They were also encouraged to debate on religious scriptures. Rishi Shivam's students spoke eloquently and debated on finer points of religion, which impressed the king immensely.

On the last day of the ceremony, when everyone was leaving, the king gave gifts to all the priests.

When it was time to leave, Rishi Shivam came to King Meghnath and said, "Dear King Meghnath, it was a very well-arranged yagna, and I am happy to be part of it. I, with my students, want to take your leave. God bless you."

King replied calmly, "Respected Rishi, I am very grateful to you for presiding over the ceremonies. Your presence in this yagna has brought so much happiness to me and my kingdom. I would like to gift you one hundred and one gold coins and one hundred and one cows for your effort."

"Thank you, King Meghnath, for your gifts. I can't accept them as our requirements in our gurukul are very limited. We live very humble lives and want to live humbly. If I accept so much wealth from you, I wouldn't know how to take care of it. You can use those gifts for the betterment of citizens of your kingdom."

King was a little uncomfortable to hear that as nobody had refused to take his gifts. He was giving a small fortune to the rishi, but he had declined.

Hiding his feelings, the king replied, "I appreciate your way of life and refusing to be attached to the luxuries of life. My kingdom would greatly benefit if you could stay with me as my royal priest. I will take care of all your needs, and you won't have to worry about anything in life."

The rishi was taken aback by the king's proposal as he hadn't expected it. Very calmly, the rishi replied, "My needs are met in my ashram. My place is not in a royal palace but in my ashram. You have seen the capabilities of my students during debates. If any of them is interested, they are free to stay with you in your palace."

The king looked at his students. All were very calm and didn't respond, except one.

Mitra excitedly looked at his teacher and asked, "Respected Rishi, you said that our education with you is mostly complete. I am willing to stay here with King Meghnath, with your permission."

King agreed to Rishi Shivam's student's request, and Mitra stayed back in the kingdom.

Anesh, Medha, and Shaurya knew the real reason why Mitra decided to stay back: greed for luxury and power.

During the previous war, Nansuki was captured and imprisoned by the three Great Rishis. All his disciples ran away and went into hiding in various parts of the two worlds. Rishi Mitra felt humiliated and went into hiding. He kept on planning his next move.

Rishi Mitra knew that it was impossible for the three Great Rishis to defeat Nansuki. They captured and imprisoned Nansuki by deception. Rishi Mitra was furious with anger when Nansuki was imprisoned. He had hoped to defeat the three Great Rishis with the help of Nansuki. He still remembered vividly how he was insulted by the three Great Rishis. He was so close to them, and all of them studied together in the same gurukul, but he can never forget how they insulted him.

He had vowed to take revenge for his insults and the capture of his Lord, Nansuki.

This time, he knew that he had to be careful in building the army away from the peering eyes. The three Great Rishis shouldn't get a hint of his preparations. He didn't worry about helping Nansuki to escape from his prison because of two reasons. One was that Nansuki himself was capable of escaping from the prison without anyone's help. The second was a little embarrassing. He had no idea where Nansuki was imprisoned. He tried to find out by sending his spies to various kingdoms, but he never got any leads. Sending spies to the three Great Rishis' cave was impossible. It was in a very difficult terrain, and no magic worked in their cave. There was no way he could eavesdrop inside the cave.

He had built his army training camp in the Dandkund forest. It was spread over a very large area, adjoining three different kingdoms. It received good rainfall all year round, and it had dense vegetation. Due to its location and climate, there were many species of animals, including tigers, leopards, wolves, poisonous snakes, etc. Humans avoided venturing deep inside the forest because of dangerous wild animals. It was impossible to come out of it if someone lost their way inside. Surviving a night alone alive was not possible.

It was a perfect place to hide and rebuild his army.

He called his captain, Vikarna, to his cabin and said, "Vikarna, we will build our training camp in Dandkund forest. Assemble your team, and we will leave tomorrow morning."

In an attentive position, Vikarna replied, "I will immediately inform our team to leave tomorrow morning."

In a thoughtful tone, Rishi Mitra said, "Send a message to all our Lord's followers to join us in the forest camp. Inform them to be careful while coming. The news shouldn't be leaked to our enemies."

Vikarna, still standing, replied, "Alright. I will send them the message with a strict warning not to leak or discuss with anyone else."

The rishi dismissed Vikarna and started planning for the attack.

Vikarna was a resourceful and strong army commander but was not very smart. The rishi had given him some magical potions to enhance his strength, but he was very loyal to him. In some critical jobs, loyalty becomes more important than the skills of a person.

In the Dandkund forest, Rishi Mitra had started assembling Nansuki's followers to prepare them for the incoming war. It was not easy to find a deserted place to train thousands of warriors in the same place.

He assembled Nansuki's followers and, with the help of black magic, turned them into ferocious warriors. He had heard about the students' encampment nearby a few days before but didn't expect them to kill one of his black magic-infused wild boars. He thought maybe they got lucky in killing that ferocious animal. He knew that such student expeditions in the forest were always accompanied by trained soldiers.

Hundreds of Nansuki's followers from both worlds were arriving in his camp to avenge their defeat in the previous war. He had set up training camps for various types of fighting techniques like archery, swordsmanship, spear throwing, hand-to-hand fighting, etc.

Rishi Mitra was confident that the next war would be won by him and his Lord. Eventually, his Lord would be able to break free of his prison and join them to launch the final war on the two worlds. He dreamt of a world where Nansuki would rule and he would be by his side.

He was elated that he was able to assemble most of his warriors, and this time they were well-prepared to launch the attack and win the war. Nansuki will be very pleased to see the progress he has made this time. Since his camp was well hidden in the forest, he knew that the enemy was not even aware that they were regrouping and becoming stronger day by day. He smiled to himself and walked towards the black magic preparation section.

He had trained his closest assistants in preparing black magic potions. He had divided the black magic potions into three parts: unnatural strength and size, flying, and fire attacks. A mixture of different magic potions was also possible, but it was always a lethal dose for most of his soldiers. For the raw material for these magic potions, he had recruited the fastest flying birds' regiment. The birds' regiment was scouring both worlds for herbs and other raw materials for preparing magic potions.

The camp was receiving raw materials on a daily basis to prepare black magic potions. Those potions were constantly given to various soldiers, humans, and animals to enhance their desired capabilities. Since they were developing stronger black magic potions, it was inevitable that not all soldiers would be able to digest them. A lot of human and animal soldiers were dying painful deaths due to strong doses of magic potions. The number of such deaths was very high, but soldiers who survived the magical potion were very strong and exhibited the desired traits.

Proud of his achievements, Mitra proceeded towards the Enhancement Section, where the potions were administered to chosen healthy soldiers. This section was a little away from the main central camp as the fatalities were high due to strong doses. He thought that due to less time, sacrifices had to be made. If he had kept the diluted magic potion doses, then the fatalities would have been less. However, a stronger force in less time necessitated giving strong magic potion doses.

The Enhancement Section was filled with the painful cries of soldiers who were given black magic potions. Either they died a painful death or became ferocious soldiers, ready to kill or die for Nansuki.

After the Enhancement Section, the soldiers were taken to the Training Section. The Training Section trained all soldiers in discipline, fighting techniques, and using their black magical powers.

The only drawback of using black magical potion was that it lasted only for a month and had to be given a second dose after a month. The final and third doses were always lethal for most of the animals. Rishi Mitra had planned to use the black magic potion on only five percent of the soldiers; the rest were supposed to fight without any magical powers.

Ninety-five percent of the soldiers had to go through rigorous training lasting for years.

All the money required to run such large training centres required a lot of funds. For money, there was a separate regiment which focused on looting the various villages and bringing food and money for the camp's survival.

The looting regiment had fierce-looking soldiers who could kill mercilessly without any remorse. They were not supposed to fight trained armies but to attack unsuspecting travellers and villagers, loot their money and merchandise, and bring it to the forest camp.

Mitra's camp was running smoothly without arousing any suspicion from neighbouring armies. Most of the activities were performed at night. The forest was well guarded by the camp's guards to hide any trace of its presence.

Any traveller who got close to the camp was either killed or brainwashed with black magic. Rishi Mitra had given strict orders to use violence as a last resort. Unnecessary killings can arouse suspicion among other people, and they may come looking for their loved ones.

Rishi Mitra was sitting in a meditative state in his room. He was contemplating the timing of his attack on Swarnabhumi. It was the strongest kingdom on the planet, and conquering it would stamp his authority on both worlds, spilling the least blood and gaining the maximum kingdoms.

There were not many kingdoms that would challenge his authority after conquering Swarnabhumi.

Smiling over his plans, he decided to rest for the night. He had a lot to achieve before his Lord came back.

His lord must be happy with his plans.

– 11 –

Seemapur

Amarchand worked laboriously on his farm, producing wheat and rearing cattle. He lived with his wife and had two marriageable daughters. He loved his daughters very much and took care of all their needs. They were both the apple of his eye. He wanted to marry them lavishly and had saved silver coins for their marriage ceremonies.

It was a small fortune in his village.

He owned a small farm in a village called Seemapur. It was located near the Dhandkund forest. Wild animals often strayed into his farm. He had built large wooden fences around his farm so that wild animals don't enter and destroy his crop. He also owned a few cows and sheep in his farm. In the cowshed, he had built a small room at the backside of the cowshed. It was well hidden from the entrance.

He had built his small house with two rooms and a kitchen. His wife grew vegetables around their hut in a small patch of land. His wife spent her free time tending to her small vegetable garden. Amarchand and his wife were lovingly looking forward to their daughter's marriage. They had planned to visit their immediate family in the nearby town to plan the whole affair.

On the border side of villages, there was always a danger of robbery from outside country robbers. Farmers hid their money and jewellery somewhere in their farmhouses. He had built a small hidden place in the basement of a room in the cowshed. It was a smart plan as the cowshed room was hidden, and there was a hidden basement in that room. As a precaution, he didn't even reveal the presence of the hidden basement to his wife and daughters.

The cowshed was separated from his house.

In the morning, a little colder than normal days, Amarchand was drawing water from the well for daily ablutions. He was a happy soul today as one of the village's wealthy merchant's sons had shown interest in marrying his elder daughter. The merchant was well-known in their village for his charitable dispositions. In his mind, he planned all kinds of ceremonies, including a variety of food and sweets for the engagement and then marriage ceremonies. For clothes shopping, he was planning to visit the nearby town. It was the happiest day of his life.

Savita, her elder daughter, was humming a melodious song in her flower garden. She was fond of flowers and had planted a variety of flowers in a small patch adjacent to their hut entrance. She regularly watered them and de-weeded them as and when required. She was a good student of botany and had recently topped her high school. Manoj, her fiancé, was her three years senior in school. He was studying civil engineering at the university in the nearby town. She wanted to study further, and Manoj's family also encouraged her higher education. She was very happy to be married to Manoj. He was educated, nice, and a gentleman. She thought that she was the luckiest girl in her village.

Amarchand found the water a little warm in his well. Calling his wife, he shouted, "Dear, can you carry the water pots to the kitchen? I don't mind eating the spinach curry with fried potatoes today."

Saying this, he laughed heartily, thinking he had leftover wine from last night. He was a jolly good fellow.

From across the hill near his house, he saw an unmounted horse running around the field. He was surprised to see such a horse running alone. Fearing a bad omen, he worriedly looked and saw another horse coming with a dead body hanging on its one side.

Fearing an attack, he ran towards his house, calling his wife and daughters to go into the cowshed. He ran into his house and took his moneybox from under the bed. After picking up the box, he also ran towards the cowshed. While running, he saw an axe lying near the entrance. He picked it up and ran towards the cowshed.

The room was at the back of the cowshed. He took his wife and daughters there and slid the box lying on the floor. Removed the carpet and pulled the hook to open the door to the basement. Slowly, his daughters and wife went down the stairs. He shouted to them, "No matter what happens, don't make any noise or come out of this basement. I will run and call for help from the nearby village. I can hide and run behind the cowshed to call for help. God help us all."

With panic in her voice, his wife replied, "Dear, you also come and hide with us. Don't leave us alone in the dark. Our daughters will be scared without you. The dacoits will not wait for the whole day. If they don't find anyone here, they will leave in a few hours."

Giving them assurance, Amarchand softly said, "We don't know about it, dear. Don't worry about me. They wouldn't be able to see me running. Moreover, I am carrying this axe. I can even kill an elephant with this axe."

Smiling, he closed the basement door and covered it with the worn-down carpet.

He came out from the cowshed slowly, and from behind the wall, he scanned the area. He didn't see anyone near the cowshed. There were three horsemen walking towards his hut. He knew that they would soon enter his house and check every place for valuables. It was good that he had built a safe basement in the cowshed. Nobody would have thought of such an idea of building a safe place in a cowshed.

Slowly hiding behind the walls, he ran behind the cowshed, carrying his axe. Amarnath was perspiring profusely. He could hear multiple horses coming inside his farm. Soon, they would go inside his house and ransack it. He was very scared and had reached behind the bushes. He was well hidden in the bushes. There was a small clearing of a few dozen steps between the bushy area. If he could pass that clearing without being seen, then the robbers wouldn't be able to track him. He took the leap of faith and darted through the clearing.

Just a few steps into the clearing, an arrow hit him in the throat, cutting his windpipe. The blood sputtered from his windpipe, and he choked on his own blood. He fell to the ground, bleeding profusely from his throat. While dying from bleeding on the ground, he saw a few dozen robbers on his farm, ransacking and pouring some liquid to burn down his house.

His wife and daughters were hiding in the basement, praying that nothing untoward happens to them and Amarnath, who had gone out to seek help.

They heard footsteps entering the cowshed, cows whining and throwing away all their household items. A hoarse voice called out, "Come out wherever you are hiding. We have seen you running inside. If you don't come out, we will burn this place down."

The trembling mother told her daughters to keep quiet and not make any noise. She knew that if they came out from the basement, they would be mercilessly killed and their wealth looted. Even their bodies would be ripped apart of any valuable ornaments.

The hoarse voice again shouted, "Your man is already dead outside. I think he was running to find help."

Saying this, he started laughing loudly in a menacing way. The farmer's wife and his daughters clutched their hands in fear and stayed still without making any noise. Not finding anyone, the soldiers decided to burn the house and loot whatever was available in the house.

They also took all the cattle on their farm.

Amarchand had also built a secret narrow tunnel under the cowshed from the basement room. The tunnel opened on the other side of the farm, near the forest. After waiting for a few hours, they came out slowly and checked around. All their cattle were taken away, and their house burned. They all cried, clenching together in a tight hug. In the distance, they could see a dead body. Fearing the worst, all three of them ran towards the dead body.

They find Amarnath's body lying on the ground. They shrieked and started crying. They heard some footsteps behind and saw two large demonic faces smiling at them. Without any warning, they slashed their heads with their sword and took away their money box.

One of the demonic faces remarked, "I knew that they were hiding money with them. Good, we waited for them to come out. The captain will be happy to see this money and silver coins."

All looted wealth was sent back to the camp in Dandkund forest.

– 12 –

Eyes in Dandkund

Defence Minister Raghupati called his trusted captain, Rudranath, into his chambers.

The team captain, Rudranath, was lean, short, but had a muscular built body. He had a trimmed beard and looked like an average peasant. His looks were so ordinary that nobody looked at him twice. His ability to seamlessly merge undetected in the crowd was an added advantage for him to go on secretive missions. A no-nonsense captain, he was extremely loyal to the king and his motherland. When working with the team, he took special care of his team as his family. He was known as a focused soldier who not only had physical strength but also had the uncanny ability to change his approach during risky royal missions. He was always called for secretive and dangerous royal missions.

Today, he was called for one of his most important missions in his life.

Rudranath, in the training field, was observing this new batch of soldiers. They were being trained in fist fighting with bare hands. No weapons were allowed in this fight training. He was observing a recruit who had shown tremendous promise during archery and horse riding sessions. He seemed very disciplined and focused on his training. During breaks, instead of spending time with fellow recruits, he preferred to spend time making notes for the day's training. Rudranath loved such focused recruits for his team. He knew that with the expansion of the kingdom, his role would increase. He would need more committed soldiers in the coming year. He was planning for his king.

He had a habit of selecting his team members early on in their training. His missions were mostly from the Defence Minister, which required utmost secrecy and competency. He selected the most trained soldiers in the army to undertake such missions.

Appearing before Raghupati, Rudranath said, "Sir, sorry for keeping you waiting as I had gone to check the progress of new recruits. You know that the new training facility for new recruits is farther from your chambers. As soon as I got the message, I ran towards your chambers. I apologise if it caused any delay."

Raghupati replied calmly, "Don't worry. I know you were away in the training field."

With alarm in his voice, Rudranath asked, "I hope everything is alright. You are looking very worried. Let me know what is worrying you, and I will handle it.

This year, our team has grown with excellent soldiers. I am very proud of their training."

"I know Rudranath. Our kingdom is in imminent danger. I want to send you on a very dangerous mission. If my worries are correct, then you must be extra vigilant. One mistake can cost the lives of your team. This is a very important mission, and I don't want to lose any soldier. Extreme caution will be required by you."

Rudranath confidently said, "Sir, don't worry about me and my team. Please order the mission, and I will leave immediately."

Proud and smiling, Raghupati had a smile on his face as he said, "I am always proud of your loyalty and confidence. I know your confidence is not misplaced, but this mission might expose you to some dark forces. You must be extra vigilant. One mistake can cost our kingdom heavily. I want you to take your best team to the forest of Dandkund for investigation."

"Sure sir."

"Recently, Ashok Nagar Gurukul students encountered a black magic-infused wild boar during their forest camp. The wild boar was very dangerous and tried to attack the students. Our king was able to reach on time, else we would have suffered tremendous losses. We investigated the boar's body and found that it was heavily pumped with black magic potion. Those potions are not easily available, and only a few people in our world know about its composition and the knowledge to prepare them. We want to know how a common domestic pig turned into a dangerous wild boar. Who was responsible for this act? Is there someone in the forest? Is he alone or has the support of others?"

Alarmed after hearing this, Rudranath replied, "I will leave immediately to Dandkund and return in a day with my report."

"This is not an ordinary mission. I want to prepare you for any eventualities. Before you leave, I want to give you a few magical potions. You might need them in the forest. The first is the invisible smell potion. Once you and your team members take a drop of this potion, no animal will be able to smell or track you. Please give it to all your team members before you reach the deep forest."

"This would be very helpful for my team to stay invisible. We can camouflage our bodies, but camouflaging our smell is more important to stay hidden."

"The second potion is to change your body into a bee for two hours. Once taken, you will change into a bee, but only for two hours. Make sure to return before the potion's magic wears off. This will help you move undetected in enemy areas."

"Respected Prime Minister, you have already solved my problems to investigate undetected in the forest. I will leave immediately with my team and report back in a day."

"May Lord Shiva's blessings be with you. Don't take any unnecessary risks and come back soon."

Saluting his Defence Minister, Rudranath left the room and briskly walked towards his quarters.

He summoned his team, and within a few minutes, they were on their way to Dandkund. They had carried all their required supplies. Not wanting to take any chance of not finding food in the forest, they carried roasted lentils, nuts, and dried spicy vegetables. The water supply in the forest was sufficient, with running streams and lakes.

They walked a few miles in the forest without finding any trace of a camp. Tired of trekking for miles in the dark, they decided to take a break near a small lake. They had taken precautions to hide themselves in a large tree. The tree gave them a little vantage point across the lake. They were sitting quietly on the tree without making any noise. As soon as they finished eating their snacks, they heard some animals gulping water in the lake. They peered and watched five large boars drinking water from the lake. Their appearance matched the description given by the Defence Minister. They watched in disbelief. Terror was evident in everyone's eyes; they had never seen such large, devilish-looking boars before. The boars were much larger in size and had large, sharp horns on their heads. They seemed otherworldly, like creatures directly transported from hell.

Rudranath signalled his team to drink the magic potion to hide their smell. He planned to follow the boar to find their camp. They looked like they were kept as the front-line guards, and if five of them were here, then their camp should be nearby.

As the boars finished drinking water, they looked around and jumped towards the dense bush near the lake.

To their surprise, they had jumped into the dense bush without making any noise. They easily vanished into the dense bush without encountering anything on their way inside. He realised that the dense bush was not real, but magically hiding something.

Rudranath was probably facing the enemy camp, well hidden behind that bush. He signalled his team to stay alert and stay by that tree. He decided to use the magic potion to turn into a bee and investigate the enemy camp. He ordered the soldiers to leave for the Defence Minister if he doesn't come back in two hours. He climbed down and took a sip of the magic potion to change his body into a bee.

He crossed the dense bush and found himself in front of a giant enemy camp. The whole camp was cleared of trees and was well-lit inside. It was a heavily fortified camp with guards everywhere of unusual sizes. The humans were taller than most, with ferocious-looking faces and oversized muscles. They were paired with various kinds of fearsome animals, each with devilish features. They were not from their world but from hell.

There was a constant movement of enemy soldiers in and out of the camp. A furious kind of activities inside and outside the camp, as if they were in a hurry.

Rudranath decided that even as a bee, it was dangerous to sneak inside and return alive with that kind of movement. In the darkness, he moved towards the camp, aware of the risk to his life.

What he saw inside the camp was frightening. He was not in the civil world but had come to hell.

The camp was divided neatly into multiple parts. He heard a lot of cries of dying humans and animals. He flew towards that, and what he observed chilled his bones inside. He had entered the Enhancement Section. He was shocked to see the cruelty of Rishi Mitra. He wondered how many souls Mitra was prepared to sacrifice for winning the unjust war. In the Training Section, the devilish-looking soldiers were trained to kill or die. There was no middle path for them. There was constant movement of soldiers in and out of the camp, carrying various items required for a great war.

He heard enemy soldiers talking about invading Swarnabhumi as soon as they were fully prepared.

Finally, he saw Rishi Mitra instructing his team to be prepared to attack on the coming new moon. It was a day of invasion.

Rudranath was shocked to hear that and decided to go back and report to Defence Minister Raghupati as soon as possible.

He had seen enough carnage in a day. He decided to fly back to his team and return to the Prime Minister. He came back to his team in the tree. Back in his human form, he found his soldiers a little worried about the magical camp and its inhuman inhabitants. Rudranath instructed them to travel back immediately to reach their kingdom.

Defence Minister Raghupati was finishing his lunch when he heard about Rudranath returning from the forest. He immediately met him in his chambers.

Raghupati asked Rudranath, "You have arrived early. I was not expecting you before midnight."

Rudranath replied with worried looks, "I have grave news and didn't want to waste any time."

"hmm."

"Rishi Mitra is planning to attack our city on the New Moon Day."

"What?" shocked to hear, Raghupati asked.

"That's true, my lord."

Shocked to hear about the Rishi Mitra's camp in the forest, he asked Rudranath to accompany him to the palace. This was something which the king should be informed of immediately.

King Devraj, sitting on his throne with the Prime Minister on his side, met Raghupati and Rudranath in his chambers.

Rudranath told them everything he saw and heard in the camp.

Keshav asked Rudranath in a thoughtful way, "How big was the camp? How many soldiers?"

Rudranath replied with his head down, "much bigger than our total defence forces. They have hellish forces of unnatural raw strength. Their soldiers are built to kill or die."

"Thank you, Rudranath, for the information. It was very brave of you to enter such a dangerous place to get the information. It's a very courageous act for your kingdom. You can go back to your chambers and wait for the next orders."

As soon as Rudranath left the King's chambers, Devraj looked at Raghupati and asked him, "What do you suggest? It would be difficult to fight such an army with ordinary soldiers."

Raghupati replied, "You are correct. We can't fight black magic-infused creatures with ordinary soldiers. I suggest we take help from the three Great Rishis to fight with the devil's army. They only can help us."

King Devraj looked at Prime Minister Keshav and nodded. Keshav understood the nod and immediately went to message the three Great Rishis.

He went straight to his chamber. In his chamber, he had a hidden safe behind the large painting of seven white running horses. He removed the painting with a lever next to his bookshelf. He took out the keys from the locket in the neck chain, opened the safe with the keys, and took out the most precious, golden-coloured ash.

He looked up and thanked the three Great Rishis for their foresightedness. Keshav put the packet containing golden ash in his pocket and walked back to the King's chambers. He came back to the king's chambers and, on the burning wood log, he poured the golden ashes. This was a job which he couldn't give to anyone else. It was too important; the kingdom's fate rested on those golden ashes.

After burning the golden ashes, all three waited in the King's chambers for the three Great Rishis. Rishi Shaurya arrived through the magical portal, and after initial salutations, he asked the king, "Dear Devraj, I hope things are under control. Please let me know what else has happened."

With a worried face, Devraj said, "Respectful Rishi Shaurya, what we feared is unfolding in our neighbourhood. Rishi Mitra has created an army of devils in Dandkund forest. They are using black magic to transform ordinary humans and animals into devilish killing machines. Their purpose is only the total annihilation of our beloved world."

Rishi Shaurya was moved by the moist eyes of Devraj, a king who always took care of his subjects like his children. His dedication and love for the wellbeing of his subjects were unparalleled. He wished that all Kings should be like him.

Rishi Shaurya replied calmly, "After the last war when we were able to capture Nansuki, all three of us realised that it was a matter of time before Nansuki would break free of the prison. We wouldn't be able to imprison him next time, and that was a big challenge before us. We can't fight ourselves in any battle. We needed someone more powerful to defeat Nansuki. This led us to perform a yagna and prayers to Lord Shiva and Goddess Parvati. They fulfilled our wish and blessed us with Abhay and Shakti. They both have joined us and have been trained to fulfil their destiny."

With folded hands, the king replied, "Respected rishi, I salute your foresightedness. As per our understanding, Rishi Mitra is planning to attack us on the coming new moon, which is a few days away. We will not be able to withstand their attack without your help. They have created an army of black magic-infused soldiers. Please save our kingdom from their nefarious intentions of subjugating the world. If they defeat and capture our kingdom, the whole world will fall into chaos."

"Don't worry, King Devraj. We are aware of Rishi Mitra's intentions. We are fully prepared to defeat them. I will go back and discuss it with other rishis. I also advise you to be prepared for their attack. Take all necessary precautions to repel their attack on New Moon Day. Ask civilians to avoid going out until it's necessary. No one should travel to forest Dandkund."

"Thank you, Rishi Shaurya. We are greatly indebted to you all."

Saying this, Rishi Shaurya walked back into the portal and left the king's chamber.

13

Different Worlds

Shakti and Abhay were sitting together in their room. Abhay, lovingly looking at Shakti, asked, "I heard you calling my name every day. Is it true?"

Shakti looked into Abhay's eyes and said, "I remembered and called you every day. I missed you and remembered our bond. You didn't remember me; you were transported to Mahi immediately after our birth. The high-energy field during your travel to Mahi might have impaired your memory a bit. You were just born in a human form. Your physical body couldn't have taken the stress of travelling to another planet. After the yagna got over, you were immediately transported to Mahi. I stayed on Prithvi. We must save both planets, and it was important for you to start your journey from Mahi. You had to meet people from Mahi and understand them. To lead people from Mahi, they also had to understand and see the real you. Rishi Anesh left me with Rishi Yograj. Rishi Yograj and his wife took care of me like their daughter. Once the war is over, I want to go back to meet them. They would be very happy to meet you."

"Sure, I would love to meet such nice people. Especially if they treated you like their daughter, then I am forever indebted to them," remarked Abhay while looking deeply into Shakti's eyes.

Shakti blushed. Abhay continued, "I was clueless for the first few days in Mahi. Virupaya took care of me so well. I believe he is connected to us from past lives. He is the ape king, and they live on Mount Kumeru. He trained me very well during my stay. I don't know if you know about that mountain. It's a very auspicious place, and no evil or black magic works on that mountain. On Mahi, I saw so many beautiful places. After the war, I will take you to a cave where we will do deep meditation together. There is a big banyan tree inside the cave. I went there with Virupaya and meditated inside the cave. It was believed that a rishi is meditating inside the trunk of that tree."

"Was that true?" Shakti asked with a surprised look.

"Yes. After we finished our meditation, he himself revealed himself in physical form and blessed us."

"Oh, that is so nice. You are so lucky," Shakti said with a smile.

Proudly, Abhay said, "In fact, he used his accumulated blessings of Lord Shiva and blessed me to have a strong body. A body which can't be harmed by any weapon."

"I am looking forward to going into that cave. It sounds so unreal." She paused and said, "I hope we will be able to defeat Nansuki. The three Great Rishis have a lot of trust in us."

Shakti continued, "We never connect with anyone without any prior connection. That's a law of the Universe. We all flow together through time; some have deeper connections, and they flow longer together. Their karmas are aligned with one another."

Abhay, with a smile, said, "That's very true." I'm thinking of Virupaya right now. I wish we could meet him."

Shakti jumped with excitement and said, "Yes, we can travel to Mahi. Rish Shaurya taught me to open portals to travel between different realms. You will also learn to travel between different realms. With practice, you will be able to open portals."

Abhay's eyes brightened and he said, "Let's go and meet Virupaya. The children of their village are very fond of me. I am also missing them."

Observing Abhay's eagerness, Shakti stood up and said a silent mantra, moving her hands in a circle. A portal opened in front of them, ready to take them to Mount Kumeru on Mahi. They both walked inside.

Virupaya was sitting with Ramdas and his army captain near the lake. As soon as they saw a portal open, Shakti and Abhay walked in. They rushed to meet them.

Hugging Abhay tightly, Virupaya said, "I thought you had forgotten your friends. I missed you so much."

Abhay, with a playful smile, said, "I could have come sooner, but then I remembered sleeping with mosquitoes in my hut. They really troubled my sleeping, dear."

All of them laughed heartily.

Virupaya was so happy to see his best friend that he couldn't hide his happiness. It was as if a mother had found her missing child. They offered Shakti and Abhay a place to sit on a tree branch lying on the ground, which was the best sitting place in the group.

Virupaya, with folded hands, asked Shakti to excuse him. He ran happily towards the forest and disappeared in the dense bush.

Ramdas, similarly, excused and disappeared. He was probably running towards the Lord Shiva temple.

Shakti and Abhay found themselves alone in the company of an army captain. They had just exchanged pleasantries with him when they saw everyone from the village walking briskly towards them. Some of them carried delicious fruit baskets and placed them nearby. All of them were looking at both with a lot of love and devotion.

Virupaya came back, standing with folded hands. He offered a large, shining diamond necklace to Shakti and said, "Dearest sister, please accept a small gift from your brother. This is our family heirloom, and I would be very happy if you receive it as my sister."

Surprised by such a sparkling, beautiful necklace, Shakti said, "This looks so beautiful. I would be very happy to receive a gift from my brother."

Virupaya offered the necklace with a lot of pride. "This diamond necklace was gifted to my great-great-grandfather by one of the rishis whose life he saved in the forest. The rishi gave it to our family as a lucky charm. Such a beautiful necklace's rightful place is with you. It also has a magical power of shining brightly in the dark if you ask it."

Saying this, Virupaya gave it to Shakti. Shakti gracefully accepted the necklace and wore it around her neck. The diamond necklace shined brightly on Shakti, and everyone was awestruck by her beauty and the brightly shining diamond necklace. Abhay looked at her with love and pride.

Shakti looked at Abhay. Both silently smiled at each other without anyone noticing the love and respect in their eyes.

Not to be outdone, priest Ramdas also came running and said, "Dearest Shakti, please accept me also as your brother. I have brought this golden tiara for you. It has a Naagmani [12]stone in the centre. Its rightful place is with you."

Saying this, he offered it to Shakti.

She wore it on her head.

Shakti looked like a real Goddess with a glowing tiara on her head and a sparkling diamond necklace. There was not a sight more beautiful than Shakti. Abhay was looking at her, mesmerised by her beauty. Time had stopped to appreciate Shakti's brilliance and beauty. There was no other sight in the whole world more beautiful and graceful than Shakti.

Shakti looked at Abhay, and they both smiled.

Virupaya invited them to their village. They walked towards the ape village surrounded by all village apes, like a small marriage procession. All apes were joyfully walking and proud to take them to their village.

---

12 Naagmani – according to Hindu mythology, a precious stone found on the head of serpent king with mystical powers.

Reaching the ape village, both Shakti and Abhay were showered with a lot of love and offered various delicious fruits. Abhay sat in the centre with Shakti beside him and started telling them stories. Everyone laughed and enjoyed his stories.

As evening fell, they decided to leave.

Abhay, looking at Virupaya and Ramdas, said, "We are very grateful for your gifts. These are invaluable gifts. They show your true love and devotion to us. We both have enjoyed so much spending time with you all. We will take our leave today and pray to Lord Shiva to meet again."

Virupaya with happy tears said, "Thanks for remembering us and visiting. I am looking forward to meeting again and never leaving your side."

Abhay nodded with a smile.

Shakti, with folded hands, said, "Brother Virupaya and Ramdas, thanks for the beautiful gifts. We will leave now but will soon meet."

Shakti moved her hands in a circular motion and opened the magic portal. Both walked in and reached their cave.

Sitting in their room, Shakti thoughtfully said, "They are very nice people. So much love, even in the first meeting. It's all because of you. They have so much love and devotion towards you, as if you have done some magic."

Abhay smiled and said, "Nobody can resist your charm and beauty."

Shakti smiled and looked proudly at Abhay.

Both smiled and looked forward to peaceful times.

14

Fortifications

The tension in the king's chamber was intense. Their beloved kingdom was under threat. They were fully prepared to repel any attack from any kingdom, but this was different. They didn't know what kind of attack Rishi Mitra had planned.

Prime Minister Keshav and Defence Minister Raghupati looked at King Devraj for his orders. After pondering for a few minutes, the king said, "The attack on our city is imminent. Let us start the preparations for defending our city. Keshav, send a message to all neighbouring kingdoms. Their citizens should not travel to the forest Dandkund. They should be wary of any strangers in their kingdom. Ask them to report back for any suspicious movement of troops around their kingdom."

Raghupati quickly replied, "I will immediately send a message to all neighbouring kingdoms."

King continued while looking thoughtfully towards the open window, "We have highly trained soldiers, but they will not be able to withstand the black magic-infused soldiers. We need to be aware of our weaknesses. We must fortify the city defences from all corners. The security at all our city gates should be enhanced immediately. The border walls should be equipped with all weapons to repel attacks from invaders."

Raghupati replied with a stern face, "We will implement your orders immediately and raise the defences of the city to war level."

King continued, "Recall all reserve forces and put the city defences on high alert. All preparations should be on high alert. Increase the weapon manufacturing for all regiments. There shouldn't be any shortage of material for weapons. All weapon manufacturing factories should work in triple shift. Non-essential item factories should be worked to complement the war requirements of the army. Inform all citizens to hoard weapons in their homes for any eventuality."

"Your orders will be implemented immediately,"

King stood up from his chair and, walking thoughtfully, said, "In the eventuality of war, prepare our underground tunnels for women and children. The raw food for the underground kitchen should be stored immediately. If the war drags on for long, we should be able to feed our citizens safely."

"Will be implemented immediately."

Looking at Keshav, the king said, "We would also be required to use the celestial powers given to us during our various yagnas. Please call the main priest, Yograj, and start preparing for the defences of the city. All celestial weapons should be distributed to the top lieutenants. They should be trained to use those celestial weapons immediately."

"Understood. This will be done immediately."

King continued to look at Keshav and said, "Finally, prepare the war room in the king's court and bring the best people there. We need to have all information before and during the attack. Our top generals and war machinery should work as a single unit without any kind of confusion. One mistake can cost us hundreds of lives, and no mistake will not be accepted."

"Understood. Will be implemented and communicated through rank and file."

Keshav and Raghupati stood up, saluted the king, and walked briskly towards their chambers to implement the king's orders.

Prime Minister Keshav called his team and ordered them to implement the king's orders. He himself wanted to go to priest Yograj to inform about the situation. This war would be won by superior celestial weapons, rather than pure human strength and ingenuity.

While walking towards the temple to meet priest Yograj, his mind was continuously planning about the war preparedness. He knew that King Devraj was a capable and strong war king, and he must be planning for all eventualities.

Priest Yograj and Yogini were meditating in the inside chamber of the temple. The priest was aware of the threat to the kingdom. He was also the keeper of all celestial weapons. Meditation gave them mental strength and clarity of mind during a crisis. Prime Minister Keshav decided to wait outside the meditation centre to clear his mind. After an hour, Yograj and Yogini came out. They were surprised to see the Prime Minister of their kingdom waiting for them.

Priest Yograj, walking towards Keshav, said, "Dear Keshav, I am told that you waited for us for an hour. You should have sent us a message, and we would have come out to meet you. You run our whole kingdom with so much grace. We are grateful for your hard work, sincerity, and your commitment to the wellbeing of everyone. I feel embarrassed to make you wait for me for so long. Please accept our apologies."

Keshav held Yograj's hands and said, "Respected Yograj, please don't embarrass me with your kind words. I am a simple public servant and privileged to be working under our King Devraj. It is my great fortune that I got a chance to serve our great nation, Swarnabhumi. While waiting for you, I got a chance to catch up with my thoughts regarding the current crisis our kingdom is facing."

With controlled emotions, Keshav continued, "Today, there is a great calamity on our motherland, and we need your help. We all have to play our part in this calamity. Could you please bring all celestial weapons to the king's meeting room? Our kingdom is on the verge of being attacked by demonic forces of Nansuki. We need everyone to defend our kingdom. Over the years, our yagnas have blessed us with various celestial weapons, and most of them have been entrusted with you."

Yograj, with confidence, said, "That is my privilege to be the caretaker of all celestial weapons of our kingdom. I will assemble all my assistants and bring all celestial weapons to the king's court immediately. It would be an honour to die defending our great kingdom. Please convey my best regards to our beloved King Devraj."

While returning to the king's court, Keshav was deep in thought. Their kingdom was on the verge of annihilation by the world's most demonic forces. He knew they were ill-prepared to fight Rishi Mitra's black magic-infused soldiers. Their only solace was their celestial weapons and the support from the three Great Rishis. He hoped that Rishi Shaurya's trust in Abhay and Shakti's power was not misplaced.

Lost in his thoughts, he didn't realise when he reached the king's court.

King Devraj was in the meeting with all his cabinet ministers. The discussions were around all ministries for war preparedness. The calamity on their kingdom was sudden and severe. There was not much time left to defend the attack. King Devraj looked at his urban development minister and said, "The underground tunnels need to be ready for a large number of people. They might have to stay there for a long time too. The sanitation of those tunnels should be ready in two days. Start the food storage in the storage rooms across the tunnels. Find and plan all the kitchen locations; those should be located around the well-ventilated areas."

"We will immediately work on your orders,"

Priest Yograj rushed inside with his four trusted assistants in the king's court. He greeted the king and said, "Dear King Devraj, please accept our heartfelt respects. We were informed about the imminent attack on our beloved kingdom. We are ready to start our work defending our kingdom. We have brought all material required and will start our yagna now. We will set up the yagna in the open space balcony outside the king's chamber. The yagna will create protective rays around our city. The celestial rays will protect the city from any magical attack from the outside force."

"I am really grateful to you, dear priest Yograj," the king said with a respectful smile.

Yograj continued with pride, "All celestial weapons are available with us. We will be training the selected lieutenants to use those celestial weapons. We will teach them how to manifest those weapons, how to fire them, and how to control them. With those weapons, we should be able to inflict serious damage to the enemy force. Some of the celestial weapons can protect us from their magical attacks. I believe we have potent weapons at our disposal."

King remarked, "Those would be very helpful in defending our motherland."

Yograj, continuing with pride and confidence, said, "A few celestial weapons will be available to you as well during the war. We will teach you the mantras to manifest them during the war."

Hurriedly, Yograj and his assistants saluted the king and proceeded towards the open area outside the king's court to start preparing for the yagna. Soon, they set up everything and commenced the yagna for the city's protection. The mantras and fire offerings in the yagna fire started resonating smoothly in the atmosphere.

King Devraj looked at Defence Minister Raghupati and said, "Call your highly trained soldiers for training in celestial weapons. They must be trained by priest Yograj as soon as he finishes the yagna."

"Yes, my lord."

After a few hours of their yagna, beautiful red-coloured rays started emitting from the yagna fire and slowly began covering the sky over the whole city. The rays from the yagna went up and covered the whole sky over the city in a circular route. They kept on chanting the mantras, and the red-coloured rays filled the whole sky over the city. Those red-coloured rays had the power to repel any kind of magical attack. Penetrating those rays by black magic-infused creatures was not possible. Those rays contained pure and pious energies of divine mantras.

The news of the impending attack on the kingdom had spread throughout the kingdom. There was a sense of confusion among the citizens. Some of them decided to leave the city, carrying their valuables with them. The king had ordered to allow them to leave the city if they wanted. Most of the citizens were prepared to fulfil their part in the war. The patriotism among the citizens in Swarnabhumi was very high. All reserve forces of the kingdom had left their homes to join the army to be trained for their roles.

Preparations were in full swing for their underground tunnels' storage of food and other essential materials. A community kitchen was being set up in the underground tunnels. Medical centres across the kingdom were set up, including in the tunnels. The weaponry required on the border walls was stored in high quantity as it was the first line of defence for the city. Wood and flammable oil were stored on a large scale on those walls. All city gates were heavily deployed by the army with their fieriest weapons. The city gates were ordered to be closed at the first sight of an enemy attack. The city looked like a heavily fortified impregnable fort. No outside force could enter the city. That's what everyone believed.

The new moon was still a few days away.

Elsewhere, there was Mohan, a well-known trader of clothes. He had spread his trading business across many neighbouring kingdoms. He travelled across the various kingdoms for his business. When he stayed in Swarnabhumi, in the mornings, he would regularly go to the vegetable market to buy vegetables. The other purpose to go to the market was to eavesdrop on other people's conversations. He believed that, as a trader having business across multiple kingdoms, he should always keep his ears open. For him, information was money. He would hear rumours in the market. He would come back and check the rumours. If the rumour was confirmed from his sources, then he could decide to make a profit from the news.

This strategy had worked well for him for years. He had become a wealthy trader and had an uncanny ability to profit from any situation, anywhere.

When he heard about the imminent attack on Swarnabhumi, he decided to leave the city immediately with his family. He knew that the enemy was very powerful. It might be difficult for Swarnabhumi to defend from its attack. Leaving the city alone with his family was not wise. He decided to instigate more people to leave the city. That way, it would be safer to travel in a large group. Travelling in large groups across the forest was better for safety.

He started calling known people and offered them suitable opportunities in the neighbouring city. If the situation improves, they would be able to return. He convinced them that staying in a war-torn city was a foolish decision. A few of his known citizens agreed to accompany him and leave the city.

Mohan and his group reached the city gates, carrying their valuables. Some of them were travelling on their ox-driven carts, and others were travelling on foot with their families. Citizens who were staying back were not happy to see others running in the time of crisis on their motherland. The citizens who were leaving the city were met with condescending eyes by others. They realised, while leaving the city, that they wouldn't be accepted back if their city won the war.

For some people, running away from a situation and saving their lives is better than standing up for principles. Facing a crisis builds character. The citizens who had left the city were moving southwards towards the neighbouring kingdom. It was a three-day journey on their ox-driven carts, and they were feeling safe in their large number. They had to move through plains and narrow valleys, at least away from the impending enemy attack on the city. After travelling for a few hours, they were passing through the plains. It was a dangerous journey as it was infested with wolves and lions. They believed that they would be able to travel through it in the daytime without any danger.

The day sky was cloudy. From a distance, they saw a fireball in the sky. It was coming straight towards their caravan. It looked like a small sun but a fast-moving sun travelling across the sky. The fireball travelled fast and hit the middle ox-cart, burning the whole wagon and the people around it. Mohan watched in horror as the wagon with the ox burned. There were a few people inside the wagon. All of them burned and died instantaneously. There were also a few people around that wagon, and their clothes caught fire. He watched burning people running away from the caravan.

Behind the fireball, an arrow came and stuck a woman in her throat. The blood was oozing profusely from her throat. She was standing next to Mohan. Her blood splattered on his face. Fearing for his and his family's life, he steered his horse-driven chariot and tried to run back. He had just turned back his chariot when another fireball struck his chariot. He and his whole family burned and died.

Then, there were rains of fire-breathing arrows on their convoy. Within a few minutes, all were dead: humans and cattle. It was a terrifying sight in the middle of the plains. Men, women, children, and cattle lay dead in the middle of nowhere, their body parts strewn all over the place.

Unfortunately, the caravan was moving directly in the Rishi Mitra's southern army contingent. They had found them, killed, and looted their convoy.

15

It Begins

Prime Minister Keshav and Defence Minister Raghupati were discussing their war preparedness in the King's chambers. The king was not available in the room.

Confidence beaming on his face, Raghupati said, "I have heavily fortified all entry gates with heavy weapons and army. We have also called additional reserve civilian forces in the eventuality of an attack on the city. Our city will turn into a fortress in a few hours. Nobody will be able to enter our city without our approval."

Keshav asked, "Are border walls also fortified and prepared to defend any attack?"

Raghupati nonchalantly replied, "Yes, I have followed all the king's orders. We are fully prepared for the attack on the New Moon Day."

With a satisfied look, Keshav said, "Also, keep an eye out for any suspicious activity in the city. Anyone entering the city should be thoroughly checked. Don't let anyone enter the city with any kind of weapon."

Raghupati asked with a frown, "Wouldn't that create some kind of mistrust among the citizens?"

Keshav replied calmly, "This is only a temporary measure. We need to be paranoid for security for a few days. I don't want to leave any loose ends. The safety of our beloved kingdom is on the threshold. Be paranoid now rather than regret later."

Raghupati smiled and said, "That's very smart thinking. I understand why our king trusts your judgement blindly."

On a serious note, Keshav said, "Thanks, Raghupati, but the future of our kingdom is at stake. Our king, you, myself, our families, and citizens' lives depend on what we do in the next few days."

"I totally agree with you, Keshav."

Keshav walked towards the window overlooking the palace ground and said, "One more thing, when the enemy reaches our city gates, send the message to all neighbouring kingdoms. They should be prepared to defend themselves." Looking above as if asking almighty, "If our kingdom is defeated, I don't know if our neighbours will have the courage to face the enemy. All kingdoms will fall without any fight."

"I agree with you. We are the last line of defence between peace and chaos," Raghupati agreed.

"I hope God helps us."

After the discussions, Raghupati hurriedly left the room and walked towards his military chambers. He had a lot to do in very little time. He hoped that his kingdom was not attacked. Keshav was sitting in a pensive mood, thinking about what would happen if the city was attacked. Although the city is fortified, for how long can they really defend it from Rishi Mitra's attack.

The city had four main gates, and all were heavily fortified by the army. The whole city was surrounded by tall walls, a few metres wide. On top of the walls, it was manned by trained archers. They also had big pots of hot oil kept on the walls to be poured on enemies trying to climb. They had built machines to throw fireballs at the enemy. The machine had the capacity to throw fireballs at great speed. They could throw burning balls up to two kilometres away. Before any enemy could reach the city gates, their defence could kill and seriously injure large parts of the enemy army.

Defence Minister Raghupati's foresightedness to invest in research and development in weapons had made Swarnabhumi the most fearsome army in the world. On numerous occasions, they brought warring kingdoms to negotiation tables and solved their issues without shedding any blood. It resulted in peace for the world for more than a half-century. The peaceful kingdoms resulted in prosperity for citizens of the world.

If Swarnabhumi fell to Rishi Mitra's evil designs, then it would create chaos in the whole world. A chaotic world without peace, only bloodshed. The prospects for the world if Swarnabhumi fell were too dangerous for world peace.

Rishi Mitra called his top lieutenants to the middle of the forest camp. His top lieutenants were infused with black magic potions. All of them displayed brute physical strength and aggression. They were trained to be cruel and loyal to Nansuki. If they showed little sympathy towards enemies or weakness, then their punishment was only death.

When everyone was assembled in front of Rishi Mitra, in a booming voice he said, "Today is the day when we start our journey towards victory. The victory would be rewarding for all of you. You will get the world's riches and luxury. All of you will lord over your own kingdoms. Our Lord will soon escape from prison and join us. We would be the mightiest empire ever to rule both planets. Long live our Lord."

There was a chorus of *Long live our Lord*.

He continued with confidence, "Assemble all your soldiers to attack Swarnabhumi. Attack and conquer them with brute force. All kingdoms should hear about the bruteness of your attack. After conquering Swarnabhumi, other kingdoms should never think about raising their voice against the Lord's forces."

In a whispering voice, he said, "Kill or get killed."

Soon, the soldiers assembled, ready to march towards Swarnabhumi and destroy it.

Swarnabhumi, being the largest and the strongest kingdom in the world, and if it fell to Rishi Mitra, then all other kingdoms would gladly accept Rishi Mitra's terms of surrender. No kingdom would have the courage to stand before Mitra's forces. Rishi Mitra had achieved his objective of assembling the largest and the most fearsome army of humans and black magic-infused creatures.

Rishi Mitra rose in the air, a few feet above the ground, and looked at one of the largest and most ferocious armies ever built in this world. He was pleased with himself that he single-handedly built such an army in the absence of his Lord Nansuki. He beamed with pride that when his Lord escapes, he would be glad to observe what Rishi Mitra achieved alone for his Lord. He was dreaming how he would welcome his Lord in the King's Court of Swarnabhumi and will rule this world with an iron fist in the name of his Lord.

He believed that this time his Lord would kill the three Great Rishis, and there would be no one to challenge his Lord's authority in both worlds. He would rule both worlds with his Lord. A smile appeared on his face.

Looking down on his assembled army, he used his magical powers to enhance his voice to reach everyone in the camp. He said, "Today is the greatest day of your life. All of you were born to fulfil your Lord's desire to rule the whole world. You will show today that no army in the world can withstand your might. The enemy is a few hours away from us. We will attack Swarnabhumi, kill all their soldiers, and anyone who opposes us. After taking over their city, you take their wealth, women, and children. You will live a luxurious life after we take over their kingdom. Our Lord will join us soon, and you will never have to worry about anything in this life."

After he concluded his speech, his soldiers started chanting the war cry. He came back to the ground and ordered his top lieutenants to march towards the city.

Travelling overnight, they reached Swarnabhumi and surrounded it from all sides.

News of Rishi Mitra's army surrounding the city spread like wildfire, and all the citizens got scared. After camping at the gates, Rishi Mitra called his top lieutenants and said, "The news of our arrival has reached, and without wasting any time, start the aerial attack on the city. Don't give them time to inform the three Great Rishis about our attack on their city."

They loaded their fire machines and, aiming for the king's palace, they started attacking with fireballs. To their surprise, they saw that they were unable to penetrate the security cover around the city. The city had an invisible protective cover and didn't allow any of their fireballs to penetrate inside. None of the fireballs were able to reach the city.

Observing the failure of their fireballs due to the protective cover, Rishi Mitra closed his eyes and muttered a silent mantra. In a few seconds, an arrow appeared in his hands. He aimed that arrow towards the protective layer, and the arrow flew towards the city spewing blue rays. It encountered the protective layer, and the blue rays from the arrow started spreading over the protective layer. The protective layer was gone in a few seconds, and Rishi Mitra's army was free to attack Swarnabhumi.

Rishi Mitra's army started celebrating, and their fire machines started throwing fire balls towards the city.

Swarnabhumi's soldiers also started their attack, and fireballs and arrows were flowing in both directions.

King Devraj, Keshav, and Raghupati were shocked to see their protective layer gone so easily. They never thought the protective layer would be destroyed so easily by Rishi Mitra. Standing on the wall, they saw that the enemy troops were running towards the city gates. They knew that the city gates would not be able to stop them, and it would fall as easily as the protective layer. They were shocked to see the brutishness of Rishi Mitra's attack. The fireballs of Rishi Mitra's forces were more ferocious and were incurring serious damages to their defences on the wall. The city's buildings and infrastructure were badly damaged. King Devraj could see his burning soldiers and citizens trying to run away from the fireballs.

The enemy forces reached the wall and were greeted by a barrage of arrows. Anyone who dared to reach near the gate was burned by boiling oils, thrown by soldiers on top of the border walls. The Swarnabhumi's soldiers were highly motivated and had full faith in their king's fighting strategies. They were successful in defending the gates.

Rishi Mitra realised the gate defences were very strong, and without using his black magic-infused soldiers, it was impossible to breach the city gates. He signalled his troops to send black magic-infused animals and attack directly on the gates. He also signalled his archers to fire arrows continuously at the soldiers on the wall. His plan was to divert the wall soldiers' attention towards defence from the attack. In the meantime, his soldiers will be able to damage the gate.

His strategy worked, and soon they were able to see the cracks in the city gates. His soldiers kept on ramming the gate, and soon the city gates were broken, and the enemy entered the city.

Inside the city gates, the king's archers welcomed the enemies with a barrage of arrows and inflicted heavy damage on the enemy side. In the event of a gate breach, the king had planned twin layers of fighting. The first one was a heavy deployment of archers, and the second one was fire-throwing balls. Both were synchronised with each other. First, archers fired arrows, and then the fire-throwing machines fired fireballs.

The king's strategy was working well, and even the magic-infused enemy soldiers were killed during the fireballs attack.

Rishi Mitra observed the heavy losses on his side and mentally appreciated the king's fighting strategies. Even without much magic on the king's side, he had planned all scenarios and was well-prepared for those scenarios. The rishi had a large aerial army, which he had planned to use to attack the city in case they couldn't enter.

He called the aerial army, magic-infused birds, and ordered them to pick large rocks and throw them near the gates where the intense fighting was going on. This plan would be inflicting damages on his side as well, but he was prepared to sacrifice his soldiers. They were mere pawns in his grand scheme of things.

Birds swooped in from the sky and started dropping large rocks on the city. The king was caught off guard by the aerial invasion. He hadn't planned for such an attack. The city started getting heavy damages to their soldiers and citizens. The large rocks were damaging their infrastructure and lives. Having no other choice, he ordered his archers to attack the birds with arrows and fireballs. It was difficult to target such large birds with fireballs and arrows. They were not able to stop the attack from those birds.

Soon, the barrage of enemy soldiers entered the city and overwhelmed the king's defences.

The king's soldiers were fighting very bravely against all odds. The enemy's demonic soldiers had broken the city gates, and the enemy was inside the kingdom.

The king's soldiers and citizens were mercilessly killed by the demonic forces. King Devraj was fighting with his celestial bow and was constantly killing all in his direction. The enemy forces were very large and soon overwhelmed the king's forces.

In a few hours, the kingdom of Swarnabhumi fell to enemies. Most of the king's soldiers were either killed or captured.

King Devraj, Prime Minister Keshav, and Defence Minister Raghupati were captured alive, tied in iron chains, and brought in front of Rishi Mitra.

Rishi Mitra beamed,

"You chose the wrong side in this war. I had given you a choice to join us multiple times."

"Don't be so full of pride. It was not a balanced war. If you have courage, then try to fight with me alone. Don't forget our three Great Rishis. Your powers are nothing in front of them,"

Rishi Mitra laughed loudly and said,

"Your three Great Rishis' final moment is coming. My Lord will escape from the prison very soon. Your rishis' powers are nothing in front of my Lord."

"Don't be so arrogant. Your Lord was caught by our rishis during the last war, and still you have so much confidence in your Lord. It makes me laugh at your capability of thinking straight."

"Stupid king, if I want, I can kill you at any moment. Your life is in my hands, and you are laughing."

The rishi calls one of his assistants and orders.

"Cut one of the king's fingers and let him know who the real king is."

His assistant takes out his torture bag and brings out a finger-cutting equipment. Two soldiers hold the king in a tight grip, and another pulls his little finger into the finger-cutting equipment. Without another thought, he cuts the king's little finger.

The king screams in agony and falls to the ground.

King Mitra laughs and says,

"Now, you will remember whose command runs in this court. You will do as I say, you will say what I say. Remember your life, your loved one's life, your pride are under my thumb."

"Over my dead body," Devraj roared.

The rishi looks at his assistant and says,

"Looks like King hasn't learned his lesson yet. Take the ring finger this time."

Without wasting another second, the king's ring finger is pulled and cut.

The king is writhing in pain. He is losing a lot of blood. Slowly, he passed out on the floor.

King's Prime Minister and Defence Minister are unable to stop their tears. They are praying to Lord Shiva to stop their King's torture.

His wise Prime Minister, Keshan, looks at Rishi Mitra and, with folded hands, says,

"Dear respected learned rishi. I have heard a lot about your knowledge of various scriptures. There is no one in the entire world who can stand before you and your wisdom. I beg such a wise man to forgive a small man like Devraj. If your torture kills him, then it will be blamed on your lack of wisdom. In your great heart, please let him live. When the three Great Rishis hear about your conquest of this kingdom, they will surely come to meet you. If you kill Devraj before your meeting, then you will lose your bargain with the other rishis. I urge you to forgive him and let us take him to a doctor. As long as he lives, you will be able to bargain strongly with the other rishis."

Rishi Mitra thought to himself that what Keshav said is correct. He shouldn't kill the King yet. His life had more value to him than being dead.

Mitra said,

"You are a wise man. Since you have a soft heart towards your king, you can take him and call the doctor in the prison. Since you have interrupted me, I will execute your Defence Minister, Raghupati, in place of your king."

The rishi called one of his soldiers and ordered him to execute Raghupati.

The soldier took out his sword and, in one swoosh, cut Raghupati's head.

Raghupati's head rolled over the king's leg, and his torso fell to the ground.

Keshav pulled himself up and, with crying eyes, walked towards the prison with another soldier carrying an unconscious Devraj on his shoulders.

– 16 –

Kumeru

Serpent king, Vasu, was the king of an underground serpent city, Pataal Lok, deep underground Mahi. It was a well-functioning serpent city with serpent rooms, schools, roads, and artificial lights across the city. The Naagmani[13], a magical gem which is grown on old wise serpent's heads, could light up whole rooms. Over thousands of years, multiple Naagmanis were lighting up the serpent city. They were the keepers of the magical world deep inside Mahi.

Vasu had a great many magical powers as the king of serpents. He could hypnotise, speak through the mind, cure any poisonous bite, shapeshift into any animal or human, and communicate with anyone in both worlds. He had learned all these magical skills in Pataal Lok while growing up.

The school in Pataal Lok admitted serpents across the whole planet, Mahi. Their most difficult training

---

13 Naagmani – an invaluable gem grown on an old snake's head which has magical powers.

was in shapeshifting into other animals or humans. Only cobra species had inbuilt qualities to learn this technique. The other serpent varieties struggled to learn shapeshifting. Serpents, which learned this technique, were automatically promoted to Vasu's inner circle. This skill, to Vasu's inner circle, gave Vasu immense powers to get information on all animal tribes. Vasu always knew beforehand of any war or friendship between the various tribes.

If Vasu heard anything relating to Nansuki, he was asked to inform immediately to the three Great Rishis. He hadn't heard about Nansuki's followers' movement in a long time. He thought either they were disorganised or not present on Mahi. Either, was good news.

It was impossible for anyone to reach Pataal Lok without Vasu's permission. Vasu's large army of serpents kept a watch on planet Mahi, and any event, big or small, was communicated to the three Great Rishis.

Vasu had eyes and ears all over Mahi, but it couldn't control any events on Prithvi, and events on Prithvi always impacted Mahi. Events which happened on Prithvi were spilling over Mahi.

The dark clouds had encircled Kumeru. The clouds were dark, with regular blue lightning and loud noises, as if they would fall on Kumeru and burn everything. They were not regular rain clouds but looked much more sinister. The omens looked threatening.

Animals were running around, scared, and birds were flying in haphazard directions. Everyone was trying to find a safe place to hide from the impending doom.

In the morning, when Virupaya had finished his morning ritual and was ready to leave for the training camp, an owl came to meet him. The owl's responsibility was to keep an eye on any suspicious activities near Kumeru. They had covered all directions around the mountain and kept a close watch in the night.

The owl told Virupaya, "From the far side of the river, there is an elephant herd walking towards your village. It doesn't look like a normal elephant herd as it has no calves and no females; only male elephants. We have never seen such an elephant herd. We found that strange and came to inform you about their arrival."

Alarmed and confused by such news, Virupaya asked, "Do you find any strange behaviour or their looks?"

Owl replied excitedly, "No, they looked normal, but they were in a hurry. They didn't stop to eat any fruits on the way. They are single-mindedly walking towards Kumeru."

Virupaya asked with concern in his eyes, "Did they hurt any animal while coming?"

Owl replied, "No, I didn't see them hurting anyone."

Virupaya thought for a few seconds and said, "Thank you for the information. I will go and investigate myself."

Virupaya called a few of his guards and asked them to accompany him. Most of the time, it was a problem of miscommunication as elephants were not aggressive and didn't create any trouble for other animals. He wanted to go there and check the situation himself. He had a lot of thoughts while descending Kumeru, but he kept them to himself.

"Why is the elephant herd climbing a mountain?"
"They avoid climbing."
"Food supply in the plains is enough for them."
"This is a strange behaviour,"
"I met Rani, the elephant queen, a few days back. I hope she is doing fine."

When they were crossing the shallow waters of the river, they came across an elephant herd camping near the river. There were not more than ten elephants. The first thing Virupaya observed was that there were no calves in the group, as the owl had informed him. It was strange, as elephants roamed around the forest in large families with a couple of calves in the herd. Maybe it was not a family.

He came face to face with the elephant herd. The largest elephant saw them and charged towards Virupaya, trumpeting loudly. Virupaya's soldiers were scared, but looking at their leader standing his ground, no one moved an inch.

The charging elephant came near, slowed down, and trumpeted loudly at Virupaya.

Virupaya asked calmly, "Who are you, and what is your purpose in coming to this part of the forest?"

The elephant leader, showing anger, replied, "Who are you to ask us? What is your authority?"

Virupaya kept his composure and replied, "I have no authority. I am a well-wisher of this forest."

Elephant leader, with arrogance, replied, "I have been sent by our elephant queen, Rani. I am the captain of her royal regiment. She has asked me to meet Virupaya on Kumeru."

Comfort on his face, knowing well about Rani, Virupaya asked, "Why do you seek Virupaya? Do you have a message for him?"

Calming down from his aggressive posture, the elephant captain replied, "Yes. It's very important for us to meet him. We carry an important message for him. If you know his location, please tell us, and we will go there ourselves."

"You can tell me the message, and I will deliver it myself," Virupaya replied calmly.

It angered the elephant leader and roared, "Stupid, why do you want to test my patience? We don't have time to argue with small forest animals. If you don't know Virupaya's location, then move on and don't waste our time."

Taken aback by the elephant's aggression, Virupaya looked confidently into the elephant's eyes and said, "Dear, please accept my apologies. You don't need to be so angry. You have come to the right place. I am Virupaya, a resident of Mount Kumeru."

"What?" the elephant was confused and embarrassed. "Really! I have heard so much about Virupaya that I thought he would be very fearsome in his looks. It's my arrogance that I couldn't see the humbleness in your great personality."

"Dear, it's fine. You were cautious in the forest. You don't know whom you can meet in these times. Please tell me about the message from Queen Rani."

Elephant captain was very calm and said, "Our herd has seen a few unexplained bird deaths over the last few days. We have seen them diving straight into rocks and tree trunks. It could be due to irregular shifts in the magnetic forces in the atmosphere. Usually, such irregular magnetic shifts are a sign of impending danger. We believe some calamity is about to strike our motherland. Our queen, Rani, thought that you must be informed of our observation and be prepared for any eventuality. She has sent the message that we are ready for war if that's what fate brought to our beloved motherland."

Virupaya sat down on a fallen tree, looking worried. He called out his guards and said, "They are our guests and have travelled a long distance. Please go and arrange bananas for them. They must be hungry."

His guards ran towards the banana trees to fetch bananas. Looking at the large elephant, he continued,

"Thank you very much for the message. I am grateful for your concern. Since you have travelled so far to reach us, I humbly invite you to come to our village. My guards will bring some bananas, and after you take some rest, we can travel to our village. We can discuss your observations with our priest, Ramdas. In case we need to take any further steps, we can work together."

The elephant leader was already embarrassed by his prior behaviour and agreed to travel with Virupaya.

The guards brought lots of bananas for the elephants. The elephants were hungry and finished them in no time. After resting for a few minutes, they started their travel to their village.

After just a few minutes of travelling on Kumeru, they all saw black clouds and threatening lightning. Both apes and elephants believed that it was a bad omen and started walking briskly towards their village.

They found Ramdas outside the temple, looking at the dark clouds with a worry that Virupaya had never seen before. His assistants, standing behind him, all worried and scared.

Ramdas saw Virupaya and walked towards him, a little surprised by the elephant's presence on the mountain. Elephants usually stayed on the plains and avoided the mountainous regions.

Coming closer, Virupaya remarked, "Dear, this is an elephant messenger group sent by their queen, Rani. They have come here to warn us about their unexplained observations in the plains."

Priest Ramdas welcomed them with folded hands and said, "We are very grateful for your presence on our mountain. I am looking forward to meeting your queen, Rani."

Virupaya told Ramdas everything that he had heard from the elephant's leader.

Ramdas continued, "I have observed a few bad omens myself. I think we need to inform the three Great Rishis soon. We need to call Vasu to send the message."

Fearing the worst, they looked up and saw the same dark clouds over the mountain. Priest Ramdas remarked,

"It's a bad omen. Something bad is happening on Prithvi. We should send a message to all, not to venture out of Kumeru."

Hearing this, Virupaya whistled with a peculiar noise. A few seconds later, a few birds flew towards him. He told them to inform everyone to stay on Kumeru and not leave it under any circumstances. Before they could fly, he stopped one bird and said, "We also need to meet Vasu, the serpent king. Please go and find him and ask him to meet us in the Shiva temple at the earliest."

A few minutes later, they saw Vasu coming towards them in a hurry. Coming closer, Vasu said, "I came as soon as I got your message. There seems to be some serious trouble on Prithvi. We should secure everyone on Kumeru. The three Great Rishis should be immediately apprised of the situation. Since Shakti and Abhay are with them, they must be busy with them and not aware of trouble in our worlds."

Virupaya replied, "I am aware of your powers. That's why I sent you a message. You need to inform the three Great Rishis about the impending doom of our worlds. They might be unaware. Only they can save the world from impending doom."

Hearing Virupaya, Vasu closed his eyes and tried to speak with the three Great Rishis through his mind.

The three Great Rishis replied in unison, "Blessings to serpent king Vasu. Tell us, if everything is right."

Vasu explained to them about the dark clouds on Kumeru and their predicament of something bad happening on Prithvi. The rishis heard Vasu, and

Rishi Shaurya said, "Thank you for contacting us. We were with Shakti and Abhay, training them for the impending war with Nansuki. We will check again on Prithvi if anything bad has happened there."

After informing the three Great Rishis, Virupaya introduced Vasu to the elephant group. The elephants looked very impressed with Vasu's capabilities and the way they all lived harmoniously on Kumeru.

Vasu, looking at the elephants, said, "I had the fortune of fighting with your queen in the last war. When you return, please accept my best wishes and convey my regards to her."

Elephants refused to stay any longer on the mountain as they thought that it was important to inform their queen soon, as the war could start soon with Nansuki's followers. Elephants returned to their herd. They wanted to inform their queen as soon as possible. The war was for both worlds. It was important to be prepared and sacrifice for their motherland.

Ramdas remarked, "I think we should prepare for the war. It has arrived sooner than we expected."

The elephant herds consist mainly of females and calves. The oldest one, the matriarch, is the leader of a herd. Rani was the queen of all elephants' herds in the forest. She was considered fair and a very powerful elephant. She kept a close watch on all events in the forest.

When the elephant group returned from Kumeru, the leader approached the queen and said, "As ordered, we were able to contact Virupaya in Kumeru. We had given him the message. We also met priest Ramdas and the serpent king, Vasu, in their village. Vasu was glad to hear about you and has sent his regards."

"Oh dear, you met Vasu! He is a powerful serpent king and a dear friend of mine. He has the capability to connect with anyone in both worlds. I hope he didn't hypnotise you."

Saying this, she smiled, lost in her thoughts. As a wise leader of her clan, she knew that the dangerous time had arrived, and tough decisions would be taken by her and others in the coming war. She prayed for the day when the three Great Rishis would be able to defeat Nansuki, once and for all.

She prayed for a reign of peace in both worlds, for the safety of calves in their herds.

– 17 –

Attack

Vasu, the serpent king's message to the three Great Rishis troubled them. They decided to investigate Prithvi. It was surprising that they hadn't received any message from anyone. They had a lot of disciples on Prithvi, and they had to message the rishis in case of any trouble.

The three Great Rishis were in discussions with Shakti and Abhya. Their discussions ranged from spirituality to mundane householder issues.

Rishi Shaurya said,

"The role of a husband is to take care of his family's physical needs, like a safe place to live, regular and nutritious food on the table, and preparing his children to grow into mature adults."

Abhay asked,

"Respected rishi, how does a man prepare his children to grow into mature adults?"

"A child imitates his father. If a father is disciplined and hard-working, then his children grow up with the values of discipline and hard work. His children will become disciplined, hard-working citizens of the kingdom. An intellectual father's children would be intellectually aligned citizens. A thief's children will learn to steal and will believe that stealing is the correct way to earn their living."

"Does it mean that there is no hope for children born in broken families?"

"That's where the role of King is important. He must create an environment for his citizens where equal opportunities should be available to its citizens without any bias. The justice system should be swift and strong to create a safe feeling for its citizens. The basic security of food, education, and health should create an environment for all children to find their innate strengths. When they grow up, they would become invaluable members of their community and grow the prosperity of their kingdom."

"The king is very important for the prosperity of his kingdom?"

"True. He should be surrounded by able advisers who think about the wellbeing of its citizens first."

"It sounds as if there is no easy answer, and building that balance is the sole responsibility of the King."

"Correct. We should finish today's discussions here. Vasu informed us about some unpleasant situation regarding Mahi. We need to investigate and check if any actions are required by us. We will continue our discussions later."

"Respected rishi, do let us know if you need us for any unpleasant situation,"

All rishis nodded and went into their meditative state to investigate.

They had totally forgotten to read any signs of Nansuki's followers' attack on Swarnabhumi. They had been busy teaching Shakti and Abhay in their cave, and teaching them took precedence over everything.

They had a vast network of disciples across both worlds. All of them were responsible for keeping the rishis updated in the event of any movement of Rishi Mitra or Nansuki. Everyone failed this time. It was very surprising that Rishi Mitra was able to assemble such a large force undetected and capture the most powerful kingdom on Prithvi.

Rishi Mitra was the most loyal disciple of Nansuki. Over the years, he had acquired a lot of powers, and a few powers were also given by Nansuki. Nansuki's followers followed Rishi Mitra. In the absence of Nansuki, Rishi Mitra had control over his vast network of followers. He had full confidence in Nansuki's escape from the prison. But rishi was unable to find its location. The three Great Rishis had imprisoned Nansuki, and the location of the prison was only known to them. If he had known the location, he would have gone to rescue his Lord.

The three Great Rishis decided to investigate if any attack by Nansuki's disciples had taken place on Prithvi. They sat in meditation and started travelling to various kingdoms. What they saw in Swarnabhumi was unimaginable.

The whole kingdom was in ruins, as if some powerful tornado had ripped through Swarnabhumi and destroyed everything in its path. The city gates were broken, and dead animals like horses, donkeys, and people were lying unclaimed on roads and public places.

Most of the houses were ransacked by the invading army. Citizens couldn't leave the city and were too scared, hiding in their houses. There was an atmosphere of total terror on the citizens' faces. Some unknown creatures were guarding the city gates and marching on the city roads.

In the King's court, Rishi Mitra was sitting on the King's throne with his disciples, filling up the whole court. There was no sign of King Devraj. They saw that King Devraj, his ministers, his advisers, and soldiers were all imprisoned. Rishi Mitra had total control over the kingdom. The three Great Rishis knew about the powers of Rishi Mitra as he was one of them before he betrayed the three Great Rishis to be with Nansuki.

It was a very heart-wrenching sight to see such a great kingdom fall to ruins in such a short time. They remembered that they had met King Devraj a few days back, and there was no hint of any attack from anywhere. They understood that rishi must have attacked them without any warning, and Devraj couldn't even call for help. They had missed reading any sign of an attack on the city. They knew that Nansuki must have motivated Rishi Mitra to attack Swarnabhumi to cause such mayhem. He must have planned something, and maybe Nansuki is on the verge of breaking free from the prison. They also realised that King Mitra had become stronger, and he created an army infused with black magical powers. Those black magical powers were prohibited from being used on animals and humans. They were known to create dangerous side effects and were mostly lethal to the vast majority.

King Devraj was badly hurt and unconscious in the prison. Both Devraj and his ministers were imprisoned and kept in the deepest prison chambers. The security around the prison was very strong, with both human and non-human soldiers guarding it.

The three Great Rishis understood that it was very important to King Devraj and his ministers to save their kingdom from total collapse. The fall of Swarnabhumi can lead to the total collapse of both worlds. It was very important to save Swarnabhumi to defeat Nansuki.

Back in their cave, the three Great Rishis called Abhay and Shakti and told them what they had seen in Swarnabhumi.

Shakti said,

"We should immediately go to Swarnabhumi and help King Devraj. King Devraj is the beloved king of his kingdom. If Rishi Mitra is responsible for killing so many innocent people, then he should face the consequences of such an act."

Abhay continued,

"If we can't save King Devraj from this injustice and punish Rishi Mitra, responsible for the senseless killing of so many people, then our celestial birth will have no meaning. We should leave at once and bring justice to the people responsible for this anarchy."

Rishi Anesh, in a grave approach, said,

"You both are correct that Swarnabhumi must be saved, and King Devraj should be brought back on the King's throne. But both of you understand that all three of us have a sacred vow to not kill any living being. Even if the creatures in Swarnabhumi are infused with black magic, they are still alive. The three of us are forbidden to go to war. We are scared to send you both alone to fight Rishi Mitra and his army. We have a lot of attachment for both of you as we consider you as our children."

Shakti answered,

"We also consider you as our parents, but we also know our responsibilities towards both worlds. We both are born to fulfil a specific purpose, and we think that the time has come to work towards fulfilling our destiny. Please show us the way to save Swarnabhumi from the evil designs of Rishi Mitra and Nansuki."

With a heavy heart, they blessed both, and with moist eyes, Rishi Shaurya said,

"We just met you and wanted to teach so many things, but destiny had other plans. We will be performing yagna to seek Lord Shiva's and Goddess Parvati's blessings for your victory. With their blessings, you will win, restore peace in Swarnabhumi, and bring the rightful king to the throne."

Abhay said,

"With your blessings, we will defeat the enemy. You don't worry about us. We are fully prepared to fight Nansuki's army and defeat them."

"We will open the portal, and it will take you to the city gate as Rishi Mitra will be closely monitoring all portals. These portals create energy disruptions in the environment and can be easily tracked. Rishi Mitra must be tracking such portals in the city. It would be unwise to go inside the city when the whole city is under his control. For fighting from the outside city gate, we will give a celestial chariot. We got it from one of our yagnas from Lord Shiva. It is a flying chariot driven by five horses, which will help you during fighting. This chariot is indestructible, and no amount of black magic or weapons can harm it. On the chariot, the enemy would not be able to chase you, and you will be able to fight them from all sides."

Saying this, they closed their eyes and murmured a silent mantra. Within a few minutes, a celestial chariot was standing in the cave.

It was the most beautiful chariot in the world. Its size was majestic in golden colour, pulled by huge five white horses. It had four iron-built large wheels. In its driver's seat, a charioteer of short height and fair complexion was seated. His name was Gopal and he was an expert charioteer in battles. Behind the driver, there was a standing cabin area to accommodate two fighters. There were many storage spaces to store spears, bow, arrows, and other battle equipment. The banner was in saffron colour, and Lord Shiva's trident picture on the flag.

Gopal dismounted from the chariot and said,

"Respected Rishis, please accept my wishes. Please order me, which battle do we have to conquer today?"

Rishi Shaurya said,

"You have to take Shakti and Abhay to Sawrnabhumi. They will attack Rishi Mitra's defence forces and rescue the kingdom from his clutches."

Gopal folded his hands in namaste and replied,

"As you wish, dear rishis. I will do my best to help Shakti and Abhay to defeat Rishi Mitra's forces and will come back after victory."

He went towards Shakti and Abhay and, with folded hands, saluted them.

Looking at Shakti and Abhay, Rishi Shaurya continued, "We also contacted Virupaya to bring his army for the war. They will be fighting with you at the city gates. We will open a portal for their army to reach the city gates. They will bring their armies of apes, elephants, and serpents. You will attack the East gate as it is closest to the King's court and will have heavy enemy presence. The East gate will be heavily fortified by Rishi Mitra. He knows the value of the King, and I think in the event of losing the war, he will try to bargain with you. Keep all precautions to avoid the bloodshed of innocent citizens. May Lord Shiva bless you to fight this war for peace and give you victory over your enemies."

Shakti and Abhay climbed onto the chariot and stood in the warrior's cabin. Standing on the celestial chariot, they looked like terrifying gods ready to annihilate the world. Shakti's eyes were burning red, ready to fire on enemies. Abhay, holding his bow, looked very calm, but his eyes were full of terror.

Looking at both, all three Great Rishis closed their eyes and chanted a silent mantra. The chariot was transported in front of the East gate. The soldiers from Mahi were still walking in from the portal. Slowly, they were filling the place behind their chariot. Soon, thousands of soldiers were standing behind them.

Looking at Abhay, Shakti said, "Let us embark on our life's purpose and save the people of Swarnabhumi." Their chariot started moving towards the city gate.

– 18 –

Turmoil

Rishi Mitra heard about the enemy army formation at all four gates of Swarnabhumi. He called Vikarna, his army chief, and asked about the preparedness for the impending attack.

Rishi Mitra asked, "Vikarna, the three Great Rishis have sent their allies to attack us to save King Devraj."

"Their armies consist of only animals and not soldiers," laughed Vikarna. "They will not be able to withstand our might even for an hour."

The rishi frowned and asked, "They have come to attack us. You don't even know their origin, whether they are from this world or not."

Arrogantly, Vikarna said, "It doesn't matter which world they belong to. We crumpled Swarnabhumi in less than a day. If you order me now, I will take my army and crush them."

The rishi's eyebrows raised with concern, and he replied, "You don't want to measure the strength of the enemy. Without understanding them, you want to attack."

"Respected rishi, I have full confidence in my army's strength. There is no force in the whole world that can defeat us."

Staring outside the window, Mitra asked, "Hmmm, what is your plan?"

Vikarna, with aggressive thumping chest, said, "I will immediately go out and attack them outside the city gates."

Mitra looked angrily at Vikarna and said, "Stupid, don't behave like an agitated child. Close the city gates, summon the birds for aerial attack, and throw fire balls on their army. Before they enter the city, inflict maximum damage on their forces."

Vikarna, visibly upset and a little scared, said, "Forgive me, rishi, for any misunderstanding. I will follow your orders immediately."

Vikarna left immediately to follow the rishi's orders, wondering why the rishi fears insignificant wild animals. He thought to himself that he is the head of the most fearsome army ever created on Prithvi and he can't fear any attacks by insignificant forces. He smiled to himself and walked towards his chambers.

Rishi Mitra knew that Virupaya had brought his army from Mahi. If such a huge army had travelled from Mahi, then the three Great Rishis were also involved.

They would never risk sending an unprepared army to attack us and rescue Devraj, the king.

Vikarna in his chambers called his trusted lieutenants and ordered, "Call all aerial army and send them to attack the enemy outside the gates. The attacking birds' regiment should throw large rocks on the enemy outside the city gates. There shouldn't be any letdown of the attack on the enemy forces."

"Sir, I will immediately summon the birds and order the aerial attack on the army," replied one of his lieutenants in charge of the aerial force.

"During the aerial attack, order the soldiers on the wall to throw fireballs towards the enemy. They should be surprised by the aerial attack by birds."

"Will do as ordered, sir."

Lost in thoughts, Vikarna ordered, "I also want to safeguard the city gates. Double the forces inside the gates, and under no condition, anyone should enter the city without my orders."

"Yes sir."

Saying this, Vikarna dismissed the meeting and called his security to proceed towards the East wall. He wanted to see the attack himself. He knew his forces were far too superior and would easily demolish the enemy within a few hours.

Standing on the wall, he saw a young boy and a girl on a chariot. Behind them, a small force of apes and elephants. He focused again and was surprised to see such a small force to attack the strongest army in the world.

A soldier came running towards Vikarna and said, "Sir, I have got reports that at the South gate, the army is led by a terrifying ape. It doesn't look like he is from our world. His army consists of apes, elephants, and humans. We have already captured the most powerful kingdom in the world within a day. But the confidence on their faces is of a winning army."

"Don't talk like a coward. You don't win battles with confidence, but with brute force. I think I am required on the South gate. I will relish killing them with pleasure. Children are fighting on this gate; my birds will finish them," Vikarna remarked arrogantly.

Vikarna ordered his aerial bird's regiment to attack and fire balls, to resume shortly after the birds' attack.

He thought of updating rishi before going to the South gate.

Hearing Vikarna, the rishi fell silent and started thinking that if the three Great Rishis are behind this, they must have opened the portal to bring the army from the other world. But a young couple on a chariot alone was something he wasn't sure about. After pondering over the issue for a few minutes, Rishi Mitra ordered

Vikarna to launch an attack and decimate them, like they decimated Swarnabhumi in a day.

Confident in the capabilities of his army, he was sure he didn't need to worry about such a puny force. He smiled, thinking that the enemy army would be surprised by the strength of his own troops.

The rishi sat on the throne and waited for the ferocious attack on the enemy army. He was lost in these thoughts, wondering when he would meet his Lord and how happy he would be in his presence.

Virupaya was leading the South gate. He was in his full army dress, ready to launch the attack, but waiting for the signal from Abhay and Shakti. After he mentally received the attack signal from Shakti, he asked his soldiers to launch an attack towards the gate.

He saw some movement from the city walls and saw large birds flying over them. Slowly, the birds started coming down, throwing large rocks on his army. They were prepared for such an attack and used their large spears to throw at them to deflect them. They were successful in diverting most of the rocks. A few rocks hit Virupaya's army and killed his soldiers. Virupaya ordered his archers to target the birds and kill them with fire arrows. The attack from the soldiers was precise and fatal for the birds. A few birds tried to come to attack them on the ground but were trampled by elephants. The serpents were not fighting from the ground but were able to jump long distances on flying birds' necks. The poisonous bites of the serpents were lethal, causing instantaneous deaths.

Watching their birds die in great numbers, the fireball attack was commenced by Vikarna's soldiers.

Looking at the fireball attack, the archers started targeting them with arrows imbued with magical powers, specifically ice arrows. It seemed that the moment the arrows touched the fireballs, they turned into water vapour.

Observing the situation in the battleground, Virupaya was a little surprised by the defensive tactics of the enemy. He hadn't thought that an animal army could be so skilled in archery. It was the first time he had watched such skilled defences in the enemy.

Vikarna was observing the battle from the South gate and was baffled by the enemy soldiers' capability to easily deflect birds and fireballs' attacks. He had believed that the enemy wouldn't be able to withstand his aerial attack, but he was wrong in calculating the enemy's strength.

Virupaya ordered his troops to attack the gate and enter the city. The elephants came near the gate, and within a few minutes, the gates turned to rubble. The elephants were much stronger than the regular ones, as well as agile.

Vikarna ordered his black magic-infused soldiers to attack first so that his regular soldiers would be spared the onslaught of unknown enemy strength.

Virupaya saw a black-coloured lion charging towards him from the city gate. It had unusually large teeth with devilish eyes. Virupaya was carrying his iron mace, capable of smashing an elephant's head with one strike. The lion jumped on Virupaya and was hit hard by the mace on one side of his head. The mace strike was so forceful that his head was smashed into multiple pieces, causing imminent death with blood covering Virupaya's body.

Vikarna was observing the fighting from one of the towers. He saw Virupaya's strike on the lion's head and was surprised to see such power in an ape's body. His army was fighting well with the enemy. There were losses on both sides. Virupaya, with his army, had entered the city gate. Vikarna decided to fight face to face with the ape leader and have the joy to kill himself. Him killing the army leader would demoralise the army, and maybe they will retreat and finish the war. Rishi Mitra would be very happy to hear of his exploits in the war.

Confidently, Vikarna moved towards Virupaya and said, "An ape from the forest has no authority to challenge me. You should run back to the forest before I break your hands and smash your head." Saying this, he started laughing loudly.

Virupaya replied, "A frog in a well always thinks that he is the fastest swimmer in the world before he meets a shark in an ocean. This is your last chance to surrender and save your life and your soldiers."

"An animal from a forest is no match for me. I can kill hundreds of apes like you in a day," laughing loudly.

"When the death is near, even a mouse challenges a lion. Open your eyes and see the destruction of your forces. If you have any sense left in you, surrender and seek forgiveness from the citizens of Swarnabhumi."

Smiling at Vikarna, he threw his mace towards him. His mace hit him on the head, but suddenly, Vikarna's body moved, and he was now standing on the right side of Virupaya. With his mace coming back into his hands, Virupaya realised that Vikarna was using illusion magic, and he had to think fast to attack and kill the real Vikarna. Virupaya saw Vikarna was visible in many different bodies all around him. Vikarna was laughing loudly and saying, "Run away, ape in the forest, before I smash your head."

Virupaya closed his eyes and focused on the noise of his footsteps, as his real body would make footstep noises. Vikarna forgot that apes have a much higher sense of smell and sound. With closed eyes, Virupaya sensed Vikarna moving from his left side. He pulled his mace over his head and attacked from the top, striking Vikarna's head, smashing it and killing him instantly.

When rishi heard about Vikarna's death by an ape called Virupaya, he was astonished and didn't believe the news. Vikarna was a strong man of tall height, strongly built. He was with Rishi Mitra for a long time. Over that time, Rishi Mitra fed him with magical powers, and he was unbeatable in the battlefield. He didn't know anyone stronger than Vikarna. His death brought little sadness in Mitra's eyes. Surprised, he planned his next move.

Shakti and Abhay, on the East gate, saw an aerial attack from birds. Shakti started attacking them with her fiery eyes, killing them instantly. Abhay was attacking them with his fire arrows, killing them with just one arrow. The fireballs from the city walls were easily handled by the archers with ice arrows.

Targeting the city gate, Abhay destroyed it with an arrow and saw magic-infused non-human soldiers running towards them. Abhay took out his bow and started attacking them with his arrows. He was killing them instantly, firing his arrows with lethal precision.

Shakti was firing with her eyes and burning the soldiers.

They moved their chariot towards the gate, killing everyone in their path. It's like a tornado ripping through picket fences in its path.

Soon, they crossed the city gate and entered the city, killing everyone in their path.

Inside the city, they marched towards the King's palace where Rishi Mitra was stationed. Soon, they reached the open area in front of the King's court, killing anyone in their path. They entered and found Rishi Mitra sitting on the King's throne.

Rishi Mitra saw them enter and said, "Don't try to come closer. I am not scared of your magical powers. I am unlike the soldiers who have killed easily." Saying this, he closed his eyes, muttering a mantra. A large spear with a burning tip appeared in his hands. By this time, Virupaya had also reached the King's court, killing all enemy soldiers in his path.

Rishi Mitra muttered some mantra and threw the spear towards Virupaya's direction. Virupaya tried to dodge the spear but couldn't and fell. Shakti and Abhay didn't believe their eyes when they saw that Rishi Mitra attacked Virupaya instead of them. Shakti, in a fit of anger, flew a few metres above the ground, ready to fire towards Rishi Mitra. Rishi Mitra said, "Before attacking me, try to save your friend. If he is not saved by sunrise in the morning, you will lose him forever. You think you have defeated me today by killing my soldiers. Think again. I will come back with a much larger and more ferocious army with my Lord."

Saying this, he vanished from there. Shakti wanted to follow him, but Abhay stopped her and said, "The war is over, we have recaptured the city. We should hurry up and save Virupaya before it's too late." Saying this, he ran towards Virupaya. Holding his head in her lap, he asked, "How are you doing, my dear friend? I was so happy when I saw you here. A friend like you is a blessing from Lord Shiva. Don't worry, I will not let anything happen to you. I will find the cure before sunrise. We will go for swimming and move around forests looking for the tastiest mangoes."

Tears started flowing from Abhay's eyes, and he began crying. Shakti came near, placed her hand on his shoulder, and said, "Let me inform the three Great Rishis and seek their advice."

The three Great Rishis, looking at Virupaya, were in deep thought, and Rishi Shaurya said, "Virupaya is stuck with the most poisonous weapon of Nansuki. The poison is entering Virupaya's body slowly and destroying the organs. By morning, it will reach his brain, and then it wouldn't be possible to revive him."

Abhay asked, "Where is the cure? Tell me where to go. I will reach anywhere and fight with anyone to save my dear friend. He is in this situation because of my friendship. I will never be happy in this life if I lose him." Saying this, Abhay couldn't speak and started crying.

Shakti folded her hands and asked the rishis about the cure.

Rishi Anesh said, "There is only one herb which can save Virupaya's life and it's available only on Mahi's moon,

Taraka. It grows in one of the caves on a mountain. Unfortunately, that mountain sits on an active volcano. Even if you reach safely in the caves, it's filled with fire-spewing dragons. The cave is their nesting ground, and they guard the cave very fiercely. These dragons are very dangerous, and numerous attempts to tame them have been futile. Reaching the cave is easier, but bringing the herb from the cave is very difficult. Nobody has even been to that cave returned alive. The biggest problem is none of the magic works on that mountain because of Taraka's peculiar gravity. It fluctuates wildly and is unstable."

He continued, "We can open the portal for you to the bottom of the mountain, but you must climb the mountain, reach the cave, and bring the herbs down to the bottom of the mountain. You will not be able to use your magical arrows, and normal arrows are futile against the dragons. Their skin is harder than iron."

Standing up, Abhay spoke with an icy voice, "Please open the portal to the mountain foot. I will bring the herbs, and if anyone tries to stop me, he will lose his life."

"Abhay, we appreciate your concern for Virupaya and know the close bond you both shared. Your life has a very important purpose. You shouldn't take any risks and shouldn't forget your life's main purpose."

"Today, there is no purpose bigger than saving my friend's life. I see only my friend return, healthy, standing beside me," Abhay replied with fire in his eyes.

Shakti moved closer to Abhay and kept her hand on his shoulder, saying, "Don't lose heart, Abhay. Let's go and bring the herbs from Taraka. There is nobody in the Universe who can stop us. I am sure Virupaya will be helping us tomorrow in restoring peace in this kingdom. All three of us have a lot to do for the citizens of Swarnabhumi."

Abhay looked into Shakti's eyes, their hearts beating together, and understood each other. Abhay knew in his heart that they would bring the herbs to revive his best friend. Shakti, too, believed that.

There is no love bigger than understanding and trusting each other.

– 19 –

Taraka

Rishi Anesh opened the portal to the bottom of the mountain on Taraka. Shakti said, "With all due respect, I can't let Abhay go alone and risk his life. I will also go with him and face all dangers with him. We are born together and die together."

The rishis smiled, and Rishi Medha said, "We agree. We knew that you wouldn't let Abhay go alone. In your absence, we will take care of the kingdom. We have to find and release King Devraj and his ministers. The kingdom is in shambles; the citizens are scared, basic amenities are destroyed, and citizens have lost all hope. We will support Devraj until he brings back his kingdom to its former glory. You have saved not only Swarnabhumi but also both worlds from annihilation. Both worlds are grateful to you. You must hurry and bring back the herbs to cure Virupaya."

Saying this, rishis opened the portal to Mahi's moon, Taraka, near the mountain, which could save Virupaya's life.

King Devraj was lying unconscious on his bed in the King's chambers. His ministers were standing around his bed. The doctor was applying medicine to his palms and poured some into his mouth.

The three Great Rishis walked into the room. Slowly, the king opened his eyes and saw his cabinet ministers around him. Puzzled, he asked Keshav, "Dear Keshav, what happened? How come I am back in my room? Where is Rishi Mitra? Is he dead? Who saved us?"

"Dear respected king, we were saved by the three Great Rishis. They brought armies from Mahi. Shakti and Abhay fought bravely with Rishi Mitra's forces and killed them. His army was vanquished, and Rishi Mitra has gone into hiding. I pray that with God Shiva's blessings, we will soon capture him and punish him for his sins," Keshav replied calmly while looking at the three Great Rishis.

"Oh! Thank God. Where are our saviours? Please give me a chance to touch their feet and take their blessings," Devraj excitedly asked.

All three rishis walked in front of the King. Looking at the rishis, Devraj folded his hands, silently crying with tears flowing, and said, "Respected rishis, how can I ever pay back for your kindness? You saved not only me but hundreds of thousands of people's lives today. Your name will always be spoken with respect and devotion as long as people live in this world. Please accept my apologies for not being able to defend this kingdom."

Rishi Shaurya placed his hand on Devraj and said, "Beloved Devraj, please don't blame yourself for losing the war. It was not a balanced war. Rishi Mitra used black magic to attack you, and you were ill-prepared to defend the kingdom from black magic-infused creatures. You fought like a real king even in those circumstances. We misread the signs and take the blame on ourselves for this calamity."

Saying this, he gave three small golden cherries to Devraj and said, "Please accept this cherry and eat it. It will bring back your inner energy and help your body regrow your lost fingers. You will be back to your former health in no time."

King Devraj accepted the cherries from the rishi with folded hands and put them in his mouth to chew. Slowly, he chewed the cherries, and he started feeling well, seeing his fingers regrow to their original size. In no time, he was back to his future self, feeling previous levels of energy, and his lost fingers had started to grow again.

Feeling grateful to the three Great Rishis, he stood up and touched their feet.

All other cabinet ministers who had survived the enemy attack came forward to touch their feet and seek their blessings.

King Devraj asked the rishis, "Respected rishis, please introduce me to your Shakti, Abhay, and Virupaya, who fought for us against the enemies and defeated the enemy forces."

Rishi Medha walked towards the window and, looking outside, replied, "Virupaya fought very bravely but was seriously injured by Rishi Mitra. Shakti and Abhay have gone to collect medicine to save Virupaya's life. They should be back by morning. We believe that both will be able to save Virupaya's life. You should take ample rest tonight, and you can meet them once they are back in the morning."

Shakti and Abhay walked into the portal and reached Taraka, Mahi's moon. Both looked up the mountain, Agnirath. It was one of the tallest mountains on Taraka. It had an active volcano that kept on blasting lava from time to time. Millions of years ago, a meteorite made up of pure diamond and platinum had crashed on Taraka. It smashed the surface of Taraka and created an active volcano. Due to its peculiar structure, gravity on Agnipath fluctuated wildly, and magic didn't work on it.

Today, it was breathing out dark smoke and little fire from time to time. There were some dragons flying around the mountain. From a distance, they could see that they were flying in one of the large caves. Both started climbing the mountain briskly and reached near the cave entrance in a short while. They watched the cave from a distance and saw that there were a few dragons sleeping inside as they guard the cave. Walking slowly and quietly, they entered the cave; they saw a lot of small herb trees inside the cave. They walked inside very quietly around the sleeping dragons and plucked herb leaves. With their pockets full of herbal leaves, they quietly walked out of the cave. As they reached the cave entrance, they saw a pair of large dragon eyes looking at them ferociously.

They stopped in front of the dragon, and Shakti looked into the eyes confidently and said, "With due respect, we come in peace and wanted some herb leaves to save our friend's life. He was injured by Rishi Mitra's poisonous spear. If we don't use these herbs on our friend by sunrise, we will lose him forever. We will be very grateful if you could let us go and save our friend."

The dragon queen Lynx was one of the largest dragons on Taraka. She had lived for thousands of years and took care of her tribe. Dragons had built a nest on Agnirath, and she took care of the nest with other dragons. She was a fearsome, fire-breathing dragon but had a kind disposition. She was rumoured to be contacted by Rishi Mitra to join the war, but she had politely refused to take sides. She didn't want to endanger the lives of her tribe members for any senseless war.

Shakti continued, "As a woman and mother, it's our duty to take care of our family. We will be grateful to you if you could let us carry the life-saving herbs on

Prithvi on time to save our friend. Rishi Mitra had attacked Swarnabhumi and captured it with his black magic-infused creatures. Both of us, with Virupaya, fought with Rishi Mitra's forces and defeated them. Before running away, Rishi Mitra attacked our friend, Virupaya, with a venomous spear. If we don't take the herbs to him by morning, he will not survive."

"Are you talking about Virupaya from Mahi?" asked Lynx with puzzled eyes.

Abhay came forward and said, "Yes, I stayed with him on Kumeru mountain. He is the ape king and the kindest soul."

Lynx, lost in her thoughts, said, "If you are telling me the truth, then I will come with you. I am aware of Virupaya, and he once saved my life or one of my tribe members. This is the minimum I can do for him. The herb is useful only if plucked during the full moon, but as you know, the full moon is four days away, and you don't have the luxury of time. If you pluck the herb on a non-full moon day, then you can increase the potency of the herbs by mixing it with dragon's tear, which I will give you once we reach there."

"You are kind and very courageous. We would be glad to travel with you to Prithvi. Virupaya will be happy to meet you in the morning," Abhay replied excitedly as he heard Lynx.

Shakti and Abhay happily climbed on Lynx's back, and they flew down the mountain. Rishi Medha opened the portal for them to walk in. Coming back in Swarnabhumi through the portal, Abhay explained everything to three Great Rishis. They hadn't expected that the dragon queen would come with them to save Virupaya's life.

Rishi Medha took the herbs for Abhay and mixed them with other herbs. The potion was applied on Virupaya's lips and poured inside his mouth. The spear wound was on Virupaya's heart, and Lynx came near and dropped her tear on the spear wound. Slowly, as if magically, Virupaya's blue body started turning red with flowing blood inside veins. Virupaya opened his mouth, and a blue smoke came out from inside, and he coughed vigorously and sat up.

Looking around, he saw everyone around him. Puzzled, he asked, "What happened? Where am I? Is the war over?"

Abhay cried, hugged Virupaya, and narrated everything.

Virupaya was surprised to see Lynx and said, "Dear friend Lynx, we meet again. Thank you very much for saving my life."

With a smile on Lynx, she replied, "You are welcome, dear. I have done nothing special for you. Friends don't have to thank each other."

Facing Lynx, Abhay, with a smile, said, "We can never thank you enough. You have not only saved Virupaya's life but mine too. In fact, today you have saved both worlds."

Lynx replied calmly, "We are on the same side in this war. Virupaya is our dear friend, and he would have done the same for me. I am happy to see our friend healthy again. I will now depart from here, but call me whenever you need me."

Saying this, she walked back into the portal and went to Taraka, leaving everyone surprised to see such a majestic dragon.

The three Great Rishis were looking lovingly at Shakti and Abhay. Rishi Anesh said, "Our years of tapasya have borne fruit in you. We can't tell you how content we are today with your presence. We had doubts about the victory over Nansuki, but today we are grateful to Lord Shiva and Goddess Parvati for blessing us with you."

Shakti and Abhay folded their hands in namaste without saying anything. They had no words for the three Great Rishis.

The rishis walked towards King Devraj and left after giving some instructions to the King and Prime Minister Keshav. The king had the responsibility of rebuilding his kingdom and taking care of the citizens. This time, he had help from his friends.

King Devraj, with folded hands, came near Shakti and Abhay and said, "I heard about your bravery during the war, and I am very grateful to you for saving Swarnabhumi. Please stay here for some more time and help me rebuild the kingdom. We need to be prepared for the next war. Rishi Mitra is a wounded tiger, and he will come back with full preparations."

Shakti replied, "Your judgement is correct, King Devraj. The war is not yet over until Nansuki is killed. His disciples will keep on attacking until the devil-head is alive."

They knew that the rebuilding of the kingdom would take months as the damage was heavy from the enemy.

– 20 –

Rebuilding

Next day, King Devraj called his cabinet ministers to his court. Shakti, Abhay, and Virupaya also joined the meeting, sitting next to Devraj.

King started the meeting on a high note with confidence, "Our kingdom is very grateful to three Great Rishis for rescuing us. Special mention to Shakti, Abhay, and Virupaya, who fought with the enemy and defeated them with their courage. We know that the enemy will be back with renewed force, and we want to be ready for their next attack. The immediate concern is the wellbeing of the citizens of our kingdom. They have suffered a lot during the enemy attack. I want to list down the things which we will focus on in the coming days:-

- Medical concerns of citizens – the royal medical team will work closely with the city and district-level medical teams. All medical facilities need to be rebuilt on a war footing.
- Education – Any damage to school buildings in gurukuls must be rebuilt.

- Border Security – Assess the damages and rebuild facilities.
- Army training – We have lost a lot of our soldiers and need to build the training camps, and hiring should be done on a pre-war level.
- Farmers – support our farmers for their losses and help them in starting cultivation with free seeds.
- City infrastructure – rebuilt the infrastructure to pre-war levels.

Apart from the above-mentioned areas, support all citizens who have lost their livelihood during the attack. Support must be given to all families who have lost their working family member. In the coming days, we must all be working selflessly to rebuild our kingdom."

Abhay, with a grateful smile, said, "Dear beloved King Devraj, we appreciate your vision for your kingdom. All three of us will be working with you to restore your kingdom to its former glory."

All cabinet ministers were making notes and stood up, saluted their king, and rushed to their respective chambers. There was a lot to do in a short while.

Shakti took charge of the medical and education restoration. Abhay started managing infrastructure and food production. Virupaya took up the border security and defence forces training. Sitting in their room after a few weeks of hustling in Swarnabhumi, Shakti said to Abhay, "Once the kingdom is restored to its former glory, we will go to Sumeru and continue our education with the rishis.

Abhay nodded, and they went off to sleep in their room.

– 21 –

Old Ties

Rishi Shivam was the most respected and well-known rishi in the entire world. All Kings on Prithvi sent their children to his gurukul. He was known to have great knowledge of scriptures, history, science, economics, ayurveda, astrology, and administration.

His gurukul was one of the largest, and students from around the world, from different cultures, studied in his gurukul. Children at the age of six years would join and study until twenty years, graduating in various fields. All children shared food, classes, and hostel without any discrimination.

In the gurukul, four boys were his favourite. They had shown a tremendous appetite for learning and were very disciplined students. They had similar temperaments but came from different backgrounds and cultures. Only Mitra was from a royal bloodline; the rest came from a middle-class background. Anesh's father was a cook in a merchant's home, Medha was from a fishing family, and Shaurya's father was a stable cleaner in the king's court.

All four of them were inseparable from one another since childhood. They all stayed, ate, played, and studied together. When it was time for them to leave gurukul to join their families, Rishi Shivam called them into his cabin and said, "You four are very dear to me. I have seen you growing together in this gurukul. There was not a day when I was not proud of you. Why don't you continue your higher studies in the gurukul and work as my assistants? I am sure, one day you will also run a gurukul."

It was an unexpected offer from Rishi Shivam because he had never offered such a position to anyone else. Anesh said, "It would be our privilege to work under you. We have known you as our guru all our life. Please guide us always."

"I expected the same from you. We will travel to Meghnagar to join King Meghnath's yagna. After we come back, you can join me as assistants."

In the morning, they all travelled to Meghnagar. Except Mitra, all three came back to their ashram.

Aeons later, Rishi Anesh welcomed Rishi Mitra in their Sumeru Mountain cave. All three Great Rishis hugged Rishi Mitra and thanked him for his courage on Prithvi.

Rishi Anesh's voice carried a calm assurance as he addressed Rishi Mitra, his expression betraying nothing. "We have prepared the inner chambers for you," he said, gesturing towards the dim passage that led deeper into the cave. "You need not worry about anything. No one will ever know of your presence here."

He paused, allowing the weight of his words to settle in the stillness of the cave. The air was thick with the scent of damp earth and ancient stone, and the only sound was the distant dripping of water, echoing through the dark recesses.

"You can stay here as long as you wish," Rishi Anesh continued, his tone even and unhurried. The flickering torchlight cast long shadows across the rough-hewn walls, making them seem alive with movement. The cave itself felt both protective and foreboding, as though it were keeping its own secrets hidden just out of sight.

As Mitra stepped forward, the light seemed to retreat further into the darkness and the path ahead became less certain. Rishi Anesh's eyes followed him, unreadable as though he knew more than he was willing to reveal.

In that moment, it was impossible to tell whether Mitra was truly safe within the cave's walls or if something far more mysterious awaited him in the shadows.

Without another word, Rishi Anesh turned and walked back towards the entrance, leaving Mitra alone with his thoughts and the unsettling quiet of the cavern.

The cave seemed to close in around him, and the finality of his choice to enter became all too real. Whatever was headed his way on his journey, he would face it—whether he was ready for it or not.

About the Author

Arvind Kumar Kadam is an engineering graduate from Delhi university and a postgraduate from IIM Bangalore. During his career spanning more than two decades, he has worked with multiple MNCs. His work revolved around financial services and managing clients across the globe. He has also worked as an entrepreneur. His interests include non-fiction, astrology, mythology, history, and children's education.

He lives in Bangalore with his wife and two children, a son, and a daughter.

www.ingramcontent.com/pod-product-compliance
Lightning Source LLC
Chambersburg PA
CBHW031540150726
47990CB00001B/240